Visions

Life through the Eyes of Sacramento Writers

California Writers Club

Sacramento Branch

Founded 1909

Visions: Life through the Eyes of Sacramento Writers

Edited and Curated by Nora Profit, The Writers Loft
Book Design by Ted Witt, Pretty Road Press

Published by the
California Writers Club
Sacramento Branch
PO Box 1231
Orangevale, California 95662

www.cwcsacramentowriters.org

Printed in the United States of America

Library of Congress Control Number: 2022913168

ISBN 979-8-218-03680-5

California Writers Club, Sacramento

With more than 97 years of work in the greater Capital City Area, the Sacramento branch of the California Writers Club has been home to bestselling authors, award-winning word-smiths, featured columnists, professional journalists, learned editors, and aspiring writers.

This historical, non-profit organization is an empowering community of writers who enjoy a warm environment of support, critique, encouragement, and friendship. Our deepest gratitude to colleagues and art-lovers who helped to bring this anthology to life.

Board of Directors, June 2022

Kimberly A. Edwards	President
Gloria Pierrot-Dyer	1st VP, Programs
Jenifer Rowe	2nd VP, Membership
Bernard Wozny	Secretary
Karen Terhune	Treasurer
Linda Champion	Director
Chris Hennessy	Director
Brina Patel	Director
Cheryl Stapp	Director

Contents

POETRY

Introduction

"Throughout the centuries there were men who took first steps down new roads armed with nothing but their own vision." –Ayn Rand

The act of telling a story, any story, is a sacred endeavor. It is the vision of committed writers who bring readers to the edge of imagination and leave them to contemplate what is possible.

Those who endeavor to put pen to paper believe there is magic in the written word, and it is this magic that transforms what they say and how they say it. Writers in possession of this power have changed the course of history, introduced societies to new ideas, and invited the world to reimagine how things are done.

The stories told in this anthology will transport you to places you may never visit and introduce you to worlds you may never experience, but transport and entertain you is what they are meant to do.

These writers—and millions like them—have an urge to say something special in a permanent way. They fashion words and sentences to reveal how they look at life and interpret their journey.

The writers whose works are featured in this anthology are proof that anyone who has a story to tell, and the tenacity to learn the craft, can leave a written legacy that announces: "This is who I am, this is what I think, and this is how I see the world."

We at the California Writers Club Sacramento invite you to join us for learning, comradery, and talent exchange.

—Nora Profit
Anthology Editor
Owner of The Writing Loft

PROSE

By Lally Pia

Lally Pia, MD, was born in Sri Lanka, but grew up in Ghana. Half-way through medical school, political disruption caused the university to close, and she spent one and a half years in Wales before settling in Davis, California.

She completed Bachelor's and Master's degrees in Physiology at U.C. Davis and Pennsylvania State University, then attended medical school at the University of California at Davis.

Dr. Pia ran the medical school psychiatry program at California Northstate University from 2017 to 2019. She currently works as a child and adolescent psychiatrist at a non-profit mental health clinic, River Oak Center for Children, in Sacramento, California.

Gateway

Two days before my flight from Accra, Ghana, to California, I set up an appointment at the U.S. embassy to pick up my green card. Reverend Mills dropped me at the embassy. "It's likely to take several hours," he said. "Just wait outside when you're done. I'll be back around noon, okay?"

I smoothed the creases in the best dress I owned—navy blue with tiny silver pinstripes. I squared my shoulders and headed to the entrance. The cold, white, sterile building, with armed guards and security fencing, made my throat dry. The huge American flag outside waved in the breeze. The biggest gateway in the world—my final stop as I prepared to abandon Ghana and join the family.

My heartbeat was like a metronome set to presto. I pictured myself in the final act of *A Tale of Two Cities* walking to the guillotine. Once inside, with the harsh sunlight shut out behind me, I noticed the clockwork precision of the those working there.

The marines walked stiffly like wound-up robots. They had buzz cuts and crisp uniforms, flat lines for mouths, and expressionless eyes that bored into the back of my brain or avoided my gaze completely. I sat with the sinking feeling I have when a I see a cop in my rear-view mirror. Am I doing something wrong? If not, will I eventually do something wrong?

After twenty minutes in line, I was at the check-in window. The attendant stared suspiciously at my driver's license.

"Reason for your visit today?"

"Er… I'm here for my green card. I'm flying to California on Friday.

"Please take a seat. Someone will call you," he said, in a voice that

probably repeated that phrase all day long. I wondered if he needed to
be wound up. Sinking into a seat and still keyed up, I waited. I waited
two hours. It was disturbing to see desperate families with squalling
babies, dressed in their Sunday best, all seeking a chance to head to
America.

The cold silences, hushed conversations, clicking heels of
interviewees as they made their way to interview rooms, and the parade
of uniformed marines with polished boots increased my anxiety further.
Each time a door opened, scores of eyeballs looked up in anticipation,
then were lowered——mine included. I watched faces of the returning
interviewees, trying to predict how it had gone. A few tight smiles
emerged. Most appeared tense. A distraught Indian woman in a sari
came out from a room blinded with tears and almost stepped on my
feet. Her husband placed an arm around her as she sobbed—another
bad outcome.

My bladder was near capacity, but I wondered if they would throw
me to the bottom of the list if I took off. I couldn't chance it, so I
decided to hold on.

A uniformed marine finally approached and told me to follow him.
He opened a door to a small, no-nonsense, blindingly white room out-
fitted with a table and two chairs. He gestured toward one of the chairs
and told me someone would be there soon, then left. No swinging light
bulb, but I idly wondered if people were tortured in here. A surveillance
video camera mounted on the corner of the ceiling intimidated me at
first, but as time wore on, I had to clamp down on the strong urge to
make a wacky face, just to see if that might get someone running in.

I needed to pee really bad.

Another fifteen minutes dragged on before a very serious-faced
man in full uniform walked in. He had graying hair at the temples which
matched his gray uniform, but most notable was the fact that he lacked
a smile. Without greeting me, he sat across the table and set down a
manila file. I saw my full name typed in large black letters. He opened it,
cleared his throat, then sat back facing me, drumming his fingers on the
table. I stared back at his blue-grey eyes.

My gut told me something was way wrong, and this sent shivers
down the back of my neck. I couldn't imagine how there could be a
problem. We'd all been issued green cards just a few months back, and
my parents and siblings had gone ahead of me. I had to stay behind
to complete my third year of med school, but then there was political
trouble in my country, and all the universities abruptly shut down. Today,

all I wanted was to pick up my green card before I traveled to Davis, California.

"Is something wrong?" my voice quavered. I tried to inject confidence, but it came out tremulous and feeble. "I've been waiting almost three hours." To my utter disgust, a tear slid down one side of my face. I angrily brushed it away. He looked at me like he was trying to compose a response, cleared his throat and took a deep breath.

"We've got a problem, Ma'am. I'm sorry."

"A problem?" I repeated tonelessly. My heart fell into my shoe. I remained silent, feeling a vice clamping down. "What kind of a problem?"

"We can't issue your green card today. I'm sorry." He blinked several times but maintained eye contact.

"You can't give me the…What? There's a delay? I'm flying to California in two days! What are you talking about?" I was utterly terrified at the finality in his voice.

"When your father applied for a green card for the family, Ma'am, I'm afraid we… we gave you the wrong green card. I'm sorry…"

"What?" The fear began to coalesce.

"We gave you a card for a dependent. Since you're twenty-two now, you'll need an adult green card. You were a minor when your dad applied four years back."

I opened and shut my mouth. Words failed me.

"I'm sorry, Ma'am. We're very sorry this happened, but there's nothing we can do about it."

I wondered what would happen if I barfed all over his shiny medals. My brain vibrated with clashing and confused thoughts that spun around like goldfish on meth.

"You're telling me that when the family left, you had a valid green card for me, but you gave me the wrong card?" I repeated stupidly. Clashing, discordant cymbals replaced the goldfish.

"Yes, Ma'am. That's correct. You have the wrong green card. We made a mistake when we told your father you could pick it up. I'm sorry." He opened the file. "Your parents have to apply for a new green card with you as an adult."

There was dead silence while I tried to make sense of what he was saying. He flipped pages, making a sharp rustling sound, probably to avoid my eyes. The clock mocked me, ticking relentlessly. Murmured voices sounded from nearby rooms.

"But… if you made the mistake, can't you fix this? This was your mistake. You told my father I could pick up my green card. I can't believe this is happening. I'm flying in two days. I don't have a place to stay in Ghana any longer." Tears poured down my face, and his face wavered in and out of focus. I felt a huge weight settling on my shoulders, and inside there was a hollow, cold feeling that this could not be happening, and I would wake up soon. I was a naked, cornered rat.

"I'm sorry Ma'am, there's nothing we can do about it." He closed my folder indicating the discussion was over. I didn't budge. He reached into a cupboard in the desk and handed me a box of tissues. I grabbed several and blew my nose. He simply stared at me with those penetrating eyes.

"How—long—will—it—take—to get—another—green—card?" I was hiccupping with all the crying and words coming out jerky. My hands shook. I placed them under the table, trapping them under my thighs. My bladder was bursting. I couldn't look at his eyes, so I focused on his chin.

"Can't say, one or two years——if you're lucky."

"What?" I couldn't for the life of me digest this. "What did you say?"

"One or two years, Ma'am. It depends on how many people apply each year and how many are accepted. We have quotas, you know, for each country."

"Up to two years?" I whispered brokenly. To a twenty-two-year-old, it was a lifetime. "I can stay in California while I'm waiting, right? I'm flying Friday. I have nowhere to stay here in Ghana. Friends put me up for a couple days…" I stammered incoherently till my voice petered out.

"I'm sorry, Ma'am. The rules are very strict. You're not allowed to visit while your green card is being processed."

"Let me get this straight," I said with all the confidence I could muster, trying to steady my quavering voice. "Your office made a mistake, gave me the wrong green card, and now you're telling me I might not be able to see my family for up to two years?" My brain shut down. I clutched my knees, desperately seeking a solution. This was too much to absorb.

Oh, dear God, where am I going to wait for two years?

"That's our best approximation," he continued. "It may take less time. Tell your parents to start a new application as soon as possible."

"But I have nowhere to stay here in Ghana, no money, no nothing," I repeated helplessly and stupidly. His face swam in and out of focus.

"How about Sri Lanka—can you wait it out there? You have family members maybe?" he asked gently.

"Sri Lanka?" I said incredulously. "No way. There's a civil war going on. It's not safe to travel. They're massacring Tamils——I'm Tamil. It won't work." I took a deep breath. My fear ratcheted up another step.

"Any other friends you could stay with? Perhaps you have friends in another country?"

I thought furiously, picking up and discarding fragmentary ideas. John and Judy Clayden had hosted me in Scotland one summer when I was sixteen. They'd said I was welcome to visit again——but for two years? What a huge imposition. I didn't know if I could ask. There was Uncle Nava, a close family friend in North Wales. It would be a tight squeeze. He already had a wife, two kids and a nephew in their small house.

"I have friends in Scotland...I don't know..." My voice petered out. I imagined how hard it would be to dump myself on the good will of the Claydens, or anyone else for that matter, and for that long.

"Good, good." He sounded relieved and embarrassed all at once and busied himself by straightening the paperwork. My stomach lurched as my precious forms disappeared into the envelope.

"I'm glad you have at least one option, Ma'am. The airlines should help you switch your California ticket to one for England. I'm really sorry about this, Ma'am."

At least he wasn't a robotic bureaucrat. Sounded like he had a heart. But...?

He walked me to the door. I barely made it to the bathroom in time to empty my bladder. When I stumbled out of the embassy into the blinding sunlight, it felt like a giant spatula had scooped out remnants of my brain and left me with a jarring hole in my head.

I had to wait for Reverend Mills, so I stood in the shade of a tree outside the gate. Endless minutes stretched out. My sobs were now dry heaves because the tear ducts ran dry.

In the three months since my family left, I'd missed them so much that it hurt. I yearned for the family hustle bustle and all the laughs. I'd already missed the way we caught up at mealtimes. Even if I found a place, it would never be home.

I had no job, no money, no school, no family, no home, and now no country to call my own. I was a plastic ball being swatted into the air by a sea of people who rejected me. Already reeling with the unexpected closure of the medical school that I was halfway through, and craved family support the most. A headache raged, clouding my vision. The intense noon heat made it worse. I dimly registered traffic whizzing by. People were getting around their normal predictable lives, doing normal predictable things, while I lived my nightmare.

I could barely swallow. Sweat dripped down my back. The heat was so intense. It was like a thick blanket, suffocating me. Dizzy, I rested my back against the tree. The orchestra trapped in my brain got crazy. All the performers hammered out the same note, and this transformed into a high-pitched siren.

I was distracted by a blaring honking from down the road. A bus was whizzing down the main road headed my way. A crazy thought took hold for a second. A horrible, random thought. A thought I'd never entertained before. It consumed me, like a flashing, enticing neon light that grew more intense as the bus approached.

If I just took a step or two into the road, that bus would hit me. It was going fast. All my problems would go away forever. No more pain, no hurt, no thinking. Just a few steps. It would be quick.

I moved away from the support of the tree in a trance and took a half step towards the ragged edge of the road, focusing on the stones and a small pothole just a few feet away. Heck, I was in a pothole—a huge gaping pothole. I couldn't look away.

The family will be fine. No, they won't. Yes, they will. They'll be fine… They'll all miss me, but they'll get over it. I can't handle this anymore.

This is nuts! What a stupid way to think. You shouldn't think like this.

Yes, I should. This situation has blown completely out of control. Nothing is real anymore. Imagine the peace if I let go.

The bus continued to hurtle towards me. Now it was so close that I noticed it was packed. I focused on the driver's face, unable to look away.

Just a couple of steps. Just do it and be done with it.

I shut my eyes to shut out the roaring exhortation. Suddenly, the cacophony went silent. The bus whizzed by in a blur. I was close enough to feel the suction of the air as it passed. The crazy thoughts vanished, just as the bus had done. I opened my eyes and took a deep, gulping breaths of redemption as I watched the bus retreat. Sunshine scorched my face, but this time I welcomed its unrelenting assault.

Nanci

By Nanci Lee Woody

Nanci Lee Woody has been a college professor, author of textbooks in math and accounting, and dean of business at American River College.

Her first novel, *Tears and Trombones,* won an IPPY (Independent Publishers) medal for best fiction in the Western Pacific region and a 5-star review and medal from Readers' Favorites in the literary fiction category.

Nanci's short stories and poetry have been published in print anthologies and online. She wrote the book and lyrics for a musical, *Hello to Life!* and produced it in collaboration with her husband, a musician.

In her spare time, she draws and paints and takes photos. Her artwork has appeared in numerous juried shows in the Sacramento area and in the KVIE (PBS) annual on-air fundraising auctions. Her photo, *Supermoon,* won the juror's award in the fine arts category at the California State Fair in 2017.

Bessie

Donny came into the world screaming and kicking, fists clenched, protesting his environment and what was to come. He was colicky and dissatisfied. Bess, his inexperienced mother, did not know how to provide the comfort he needed.

Right before Donny's birth, his father scraped together enough money for a down payment on a tiny house, or "shack" as his mother called it, surrounded by cornfields in every direction. It came complete with an outhouse and a coal-burning stove that belched black, thick smoke onto the low ceiling and walls.

Bess felt abandoned when her husband took a job in a manufacturing plant in Chicago, 100 miles north, to pay for the shack. He boarded a Greyhound bus every Sunday night and returned home late on Friday evenings.

While the country experienced a catastrophic economic collapse in 1929, there was a unexpected catastrophe of a different nature in Donny's family. A small sliver of steel from the assembly line flew into the eye of his young father who, after a visit with the company doctor, boarded the bus home for the last time. Within days, blood poisoning took his life. He died in his wife's arms.

Bess was consumed by grief, and sat for hours at a time, sobbing, clinging to her boy. "Oh, Donny, Donny. What will we do?" she whispered to him. She stuffed her grief into the hole in her heart while she pondered how she would support the two of them. With only an eighth-grade education, she was glad to get work cleaning houses. Her employers and the people she had grown up with, allowed her to bring Donny along with her.

Bess knew her boy was suffering too but didn't know how to make up for the loss of his father. She was dismayed and embarrassed when he took to throwing himself onto the floor in a raging tantrum whenever he didn't get his way. However, she made excuses for him; she felt like doing the same thing.

For the next ten years, Donny was with her when he wasn't in school. They played checkers and Monopoly and listened to *The Lone Ranger* and *The Shadow* on the radio. Bess didn't realize she was lonely for male companionship until she got a job waitressing and a charismatic, good-looking Frank ambled into the restaurant, straddled a stool, and called her, "Hon." His thick, wavy hair was brushed straight back. Behind his round glasses were intense blue eyes whose gaze caught hers and didn't let go. She felt a tug in her heart that had been absent for a long time.

She was smitten and didn't realize Frank was, as they say, an old-fashioned rolling stone. She was swept away, praying nightly she wouldn't get pregnant when they made love in the back seat of his new Cadillac. She ignored nagging doubts: "Why doesn't Frank invite me to his house? Why does he ignore my son? He tells me he loves me, but . . ."

Donny noticed the brightening of his mother's mood. She gave him a big smile and a hug when he came home from school. She swayed her body to the music and sang along to "Happy Days" and "In the Mood for Love" when they were listening to the radio. Donny sang along with her and played his pretend guitar. He was conflicted about her new-found happiness that excluded him. He couldn't put his finger on all the reasons for his unease but he didn't like it that Frank never spent time with his mother at home and never bothered to get to know him, her only child.

His feelings about Frank were confirmed when he was waiting in the diner for Bess's shift to end. Sitting in a booth by himself, he overheard town gossips:

"I suppose you heard Bessie's lover-boy is ditching her."

"Got some other woman's what I heard."

"Poor Bessie. She's so trusting and now she'll be left all alone with just that teenage kid of hers."

"Some guts, that guy."

Donny covered his ears and ran outside, never mentioning what he overheard.

A year into their courtship, Bess was at least four months along. She garnered the courage to tell Frank, expecting him to do the right thing.

"Oh, Bessie. Bessie. This is not good news," he said.

"I was hoping that . . . ."

"I shoulda told you, Bessie. I shoulda."

"Told me what, Frank?"

"I shoulda told you about my wife. I shoulda told you about my kids—four of them."

Bess stared at him, clenched her fists. Her face contorted. Her body stiffened. Tears spilled onto her cheeks.

"Bessie. Bessie. I'm sorry. So sorry. But what do you expect me to do?"

What could he do? It turned out, Frank filed for divorce and moved out West with yet another woman.

This was the 40s, a time when, if you were an unmarried woman, it was shameful to get pregnant. If you were out walking, otherwise friendly people would leave the sidewalk and cross the street to avoid having to say something to you. Thus, Bess never left her tiny house once she started to show, but everybody knew anyway. Telephone party lines buzzed constantly. People sat on their front porches pretending to listen to the radio, all the while watching what everybody else was doing and where they were going.

When Bess was just weeks away from giving birth, Frank stopped by on his way to California. Bess stood by the front door with Donny at her side. She felt something break deep inside when Frank said, "Damn it, woman. I didn't promise you nothing. I'm offering you some money, here. Take it."

Bess could see Frank's about-to-be wife waiting in the Cadillac, the familiar back seat piled high with luggage. Donny watched as his mother suffered the indignation.

"I don't want anything from you. Just go and leave me alone." She slapped the money out of his hand.

Frank shrugged his shoulders and watched the bills float to the ground before he turned and walked away. He climbed into his car and without looking back, headed west.

Donny gathered up the money and tucked it into his mother's closed fist.

When Bess was ready to deliver, she stood by the front window, her fingers making little holes in the lace curtain. When her contractions started, she grasped her belly, bent slightly, but didn't cry out. Just as Donny returned home from school and stepped through the front door, her water broke.

He was embarrassed, mortified even. He could see she was embarrassed having it happen in front of him. She motioned for him to help her to bed, asked him to bring some towels, a chamber pot, and a nightgown. Then she flicked her wrist toward the door and said, "Go on. You can leave me alone now."

Donny waited nearby for the next few hours as she suffered the pains of childbirth. At some point between contractions, he heard, "Go next door to the neighbor and call the doctor. Tell him I need him bad."

Donny hesitated, as he disliked admitting they couldn't afford a phone. He was embarrassed to talk to the doctor with nosy neighbors listening. Dejected, he left her bedside, sloshed through the leaves to the neighbor's house and rapped on the door. Head down, he said, "I know it's late, but my mom's real sick. Can I use your phone to call the doctor?"

The neighbors stood nearby as Donny talked to the doctor. They knew well his mother's situation.

"You sure it can't wait 'til morning, son?"

Donny wanted to scream and run out of that house but held tightly to his composure. "My mother says she needs you bad, so please come right away." He hung up the phone before the doctor could ask anything else and ignored the neighbors' offers to help as he ran for the front door.

Donny let the doctor in, waited in the next room until he heard, "I need some help here." The doctor was fussing with the sheets, wet and bloody. When they rolled his mother over, she cried out. Donny's gut seized, his heart pounded, tears rolled from his eyes. "Get some clean sheets," he was told. "Hurry on."

Donny couldn't find clean sheets. He picked up a clean towel and brought it to the doctor whose hands were tugging on the baby's head. Finally, there she was, oxygen deprived and blue as the early morning sky. The doctor wrapped the baby in a towel and laid a little girl in Bess's arms.

"Well, now. It's late Bessie, and there's forms here to fill out. What name shall I put down here for the baby's father?"

Bess blinked back tears, turned her head away from him. He wrote "Unknown" on the line where the father's name should have appeared.

"And do we have a name for your little girl?"

"Name her after me."

"Bessie it is."

"No, doctor. Name her Patsy, for what I am."

Bess had even less money now that she had two kids to support.

She suffered the humiliation of having to ask for welfare, and Donny suffered a similar humiliation when she sent him to the bread lines to get whatever he could and bring it home. He earned the nickname, "Soupy," which he hated. It stuck all through high school until he lied about his age and joined the Navy in 1944.

He had no place to go to except to go come home when he was on leave. He shared very little that was personal with Bess but enjoyed playing his guitar and singing for her. He loved World War II songs. *Praise the Lord and Pass the Ammunition* and *The White Cliffs of Dover*. Bess was proud that he could sing so well, brushed the tears from her eyes when he sang *Danny Boy* in his sweet, tenor voice. "But if ye come and all the flowers are dying. If I am dead, as dead I well may be."

Then he'd start his boozing. The demons would take hold. His newly acquired knowledge of electronics guided him as he somehow attached the radio to the iron to amplify the sound. At full volume, he listened to Holy-roller preachers from Nashville scream and shout, "Praise the Lord," and "Hallelujah, Brother!" Donny answered them by letting loose with a chilling, demonic laugh. He spit curses at Jesus Christ all throughout the long, miserable nights, torturing his mother and sister.

Donny re-enlisted as long as they'd have him, but when Patsy was in high school, he received a medical discharge. "Paranoid schizophrenia," the papers said, and he voluntarily checked himself into a mental hospital. Every month, on the day his disability check appeared in the mail, he'd leave the psychiatrists, the hospital and AA meetings, and stock up on booze. He would stay with his mother and sister until the money ran out, then return to the hospital for a free ride until the next check arrived.

Some nights, with drawn fist he'd threaten Bess, or smash what little furniture she had. He would laugh wildly and toss the splintered wood into that smoke-belching, coal-burning stove before finally succumbing to a booze-induced stupor on the rat-eaten sofa. He'd puke and piss his pants, soil the couch, and wake up mean.

Patsy wanted to quit high school, get as far away from him as possible. Bess was conflicted about what to tell her daughter to do. When she was trying to give advice, Donny strong-armed his way into their conversation.

"You listen to me, little sister. You better not even think about not graduating from high school. I won't allow it."

He raved on, the broken vessels in his nose getting redder. "Don't you have good grades? Don't you want to make something of yourself, for God's sake?"

Donny held his bottle of cheap Mogen David wine to his face before he continued, "Or do you want to wind up a crazy drunk like me?"

Then he laughed, the demon pouring out of him. He finished his tirade threatening to make his little sister miserable if she again brought up quitting high school.

Patsy was already miserable. She never got a decent night's sleep when Donny was home. She slunk to school in the morning when her brother's drunk and disorderly conduct was front page news in the local paper—which Donny dubbed *The Daily Asswipe*. She graduated in 1957. The paper published her picture along with a graduation announcement and an article saying she was the first in the family to earn a scholarship and go to college.

When Patsy completed her studies and got a teaching credential, she, like her daddy 21 years earlier, headed for California. She wanted to get as far away from Donny as she could. She didn't consciously think about him but held on to all the ugly memories from her childhood. The violent, drunken scenes were always just below the surface of her mind.

Bess remained in her shack and augmented her meager welfare check by cleaning of other people's toilets, windows, and floors. She still made excuses for Donny and was ever protective of him. He stayed with her more often than not. He never maintained a steady job and his drinking raged on.

After Patsy had been teaching for almost two years, she received a call from an inconsolable Bess who told her Donny's body had been fished out of Lake Michigan. He was unidentifiable except for his dental work. Most likely he was murdered.

Bess went on to tell Patsy that in Donny's abandoned Studebaker was just a few things: a six-pack with four missing Pabst Blue Ribbon beers, a wallet with ID but no money, and a letter from the VA hospital inquiring as to his whereabouts.

Also in the car, Bess continued tearfully, was the folded, worn newspaper article with Patsy's picture and high school graduation announcement. In the margin, were written, "my little sister."

By Jenifer Rowe

Jenifer Rowe writes short stories, essays, and memoir. Her work has been published in *Scarlet Leaf Review*, *Crack the Spine*, *Wildflower Muse*, *Liars League NYC*, the *Sacramento Bee*, and the 2018 and 2019 issues of *California Literary Review.*

She earned finalist distinction in the New Millennium Writings 46th Literary Awards.

Jenifer is a board member of California Writers Club, Sacramento.

She lives in El Dorado Hills with her partner Richard.

Her first novel *Unexpected Findings* earned finalist distinction in the 2021 Next Generation Indie Book Awards.

Ice Storm

Damn that woman, where's the milk?" Norman slammed the refrigerator door, rattling the jars and bottles inside and releasing a gust of air. The disturbance caused his bathrobe to flutter around his bony calves like a flag in a breeze. "Can't leave a man in peace," he muttered. "Always sticking her nose in my business."

Norman didn't like his cleaning lady. She was bossy and grim, and her plain face matched her personality. Her name was Sylvia Something-Or-Other, no family he'd ever heard of before, which to his mind was suspect enough in this small town. These days she came around every Tuesday morning, at the insistence of his daughters. Norman figured he was doing just fine without her, but Ginny and Pam insisted he needed some help now that their mother had passed on. He disagreed. So, what if he let the milk spoil once in a while? True, he couldn't read the expiration date too well anymore, but was that going to kill him? And he could still handle a broom, thank you.

Ginny had asked him why he minded a weekly cleaning so much, but she missed the point. What Norman hated most about Sylvia was how she put on airs. She was a constant, painful reminder of his advancing age. "Mr. Peterson, I'm your caretaker," she liked to tell him. Did that give her the right to rummage through his dresser drawers, re-hang the wrinkled shirts in his closet, clear out his refrigerator? Hell, no.

So here it was, Wednesday morning and no milk, all because of her taking liberties with his household. Now, he'd have to drink his coffee black while he read the morning paper. He pulled his bathrobe tighter around his waist and opened the front door. Stepping onto the porch, he stopped short and caught his breath as he faced an unfamiliar world.

While he'd been tucked in his bed and sleeping the night away, an ice storm silently coated the town with a sculpture worthy of Swarovski. Now he beheld, to his wonder, that each individual twig on every bare tree was encased within a clear layer of transparent glass. The chilled morning sun bounced off multiple surfaces, setting the frozen landscape on fire under a cloudless blue sky. He stared in amazement for a few long moments until the cold reminded him of where he was. Edging his way slowly down the slick walkway to retrieve the newspaper, he had to shade his eyes against the reflective brilliance surrounding him.

The crystalline scene sent him back instantly to an early spring day in college when classes had closed because of just such a storm. He'd spent that day in the student union at the bottom of Bascom Hill shooting pool with his buddies and flirting with the girl at the coffee counter, Marie. She laughed when he lied that he was the most popular man on campus. She completely captured him with her curly black hair and snapping green eyes, and he felt like a special holiday had been declared just for them.

After that icy day, he called on Marie regularly. She was studying literature, which Norman privately thought was a waste of time. For him, facts were what mattered. Engineering was a good solid field where a man could accomplish something. He had no use for philosophy or religion or make-believe stories. But he was a gentleman who liked pretty girls, and he treated Marie like royalty, then and ever after.

Smiling at the memory, unaware of the piece of ice nestled secretly under his slipper heel, he climbed back up the front steps with the paper tucked under his arm. As he shut the door and turned toward the kitchen, his foot went out beneath him, and he landed with a loud crack on the hardwood floor. Grunting as he strained to sit up, he found he could only raise his head a little off the floor. Pain engulfed him with every attempted movement.

He looked over to where the telephone sat on a desk ten feet away. Okay, he'd crawl to the desk and call for help. At that moment, the phone began to ring. Norman rolled to his side and tried to tuck his legs so he could turn over onto his stomach with his knees under him. Nothing happened. He set his jaw and tried to push with his arms to right himself. The phone rang on. Norman lay flapping as uselessly as a trout reeled into a boat. When the ringing finally stopped, he relaxed his arms, sighing with a mixture of chagrin and exhaustion.

His daughters worried about just such an event. "What if you fall?"

they'd asked. "Who's going to check on you?" It wouldn't be either of them. Each lived on opposite coasts a whole day's travel from here—not what he and Marie had anticipated. The family had been close when they were growing up with Sunday dinners at the grandparents' and weekend camping trips. It was still a puzzle to him how those girls could prefer to live so far away. They claimed that Wisconsin was too "provincial," whatever the hell that was supposed to mean. Boring, was what he figured they were really saying.

Norman, you have to get up, he told himself, clenching his teeth. If he didn't get himself out of this scrape, they'd send him off to assisted living. He had fought tooth and nail not to be packed off with all those fossils and their walkers. He couldn't stand bingo, and he'd die of boredom. Then they'd all be sorry, for sure. Give him a Friday night at the Silver Lake Tavern instead, eating fish and drinking beer and hobnobbing with whoever came in the door. After all, he still had his driver's license—thanks in no small part to his good buddy Dr. Bob, who'd told the sheriff that old Norm could still see well enough behind the wheel.

He lay on the floor, trying to think what he ought to do. As the morning wore on, he was conscious of being thirsty, and yet he peed himself twice. The pain had grown in magnitude until it was fully in charge. It was a predator gnawing at him with sharp teeth. Finally, he passed out. He partially regained consciousness from time to time, thinking once that he saw Marie tsk-tsking about the mess on the floor. She had always taken such good care of things, never a hair out of place. He felt apologetic and tried to say so, but it was too difficult, and he lost the will.

She was brighter than he was, though he would never have admitted it. Nor would she have claimed it. She was good about keeping the peace between them. Lately, he'd been thinking how much she really was capable of doing. She raised their daughters with little help from him, sewing their clothes, feeding them all from the vegetable garden—whose harvest she canned—and even making the quilts on their beds with scraps from worn-out school dresses. And always she wrote in secret, she thought. But he knew. She probably feared that he would laugh at her, so she kept her stories tucked away in the back of her closet. It was only after she was gone that he dared to read some of them.

The morning that Marie couldn't remember how to make coffee was the beginning of the end. He knew it in that moment. She would cry when she realized the enormity of it, and as he folded her into his arms, he felt his knees might buckle if he didn't hold onto her. The idea of losing this bright, capable woman bit by bit, while she stood before him, was an injustice that made him scream inwardly with rage. He had stubbornly stayed alive all this time since, expressly so he could see her to the end.

Marie slowly faded from view. Had she been there? Norman didn't know for sure. He was motionless, rooted to the spot and suspended in time as day slowly turned to dusk. Dying now wouldn't be so bad, he thought. He was no longer feeling too much pain, and it wouldn't be hard to just drift off. He didn't have much to go on for anymore without Marie, he knew that perfectly well. Just more loneliness and frailty, nothing really worth fighting for.

The putrid puddle he lay in reached his senses at least once upon regaining consciousness. *My God, what a filthy mess.* During one such resurrection, he remembered the First Responder bracelet he wore. He'd always seen it as, yet another indignity foisted on him by his worrying daughters. Part of him hated to do it, but he really did not want to be found dead in a pool of piss and vomit. So, he pressed the button that sent a silent alarm off to whoever watched for such things. Then he slipped away again into blessed unconsciousness.

When he swam out of his fog one last time, he saw Sylvia's sober face peering down at him. She was issuing directives to the paramedics, who scraped him up off the floor and onto a gurney. Better this than dead, he figured with a resigned sigh. He knew as soon as she had him packed into the ambulance, she'd turn to cleaning the place up. Soon it would be as tidy as a motel room, and just about as welcoming. He could almost smell the disinfectant.

By Marcia Ehlinger

Marcia Ehinger, M.D., is a California native and recently retired physician (pediatrics, women's health, medical genetics), who has been scribbling since she was a small child.

Her interests in poetry and fiction were mostly pushed to the background while writing, editing, and publishing in the medicine and public health fields took precedence.

Now, she is concentrating on her series of stories set in a dystopian world and on the website to accompany her work. She also continues to write poems and research intriguing topics for historical fiction and memoir.

In 2020, she participated in NaNoWriMo (National Novel Writing Month). She served as one of the Sacramento Writers anthology team members, while sending short works to the online magazine, *California Update* (caupdate.com).

For more than three years, she has also been the content editor of the CWC newsletter, *Sacramento Writer.*

Hitting a Snag

One college summer break I volunteered at a hospital and school complex in a remote area of Nicaragua. The hospital and nursing school were near the Rio Coco which separates Nicaragua from Honduras. Most travel was done by dugout canoe or other small boats. Some people walked long distances or shared rides in the few bald-tired cars and trucks that traveled the local roadways or squeezed onto a piki-piki; a small motorcycle named so because of the sound it made.

Everyday life was different from suburban California. The area was tropical, and the amount of greenery was striking. Most people lived in small wooden houses perched on stilts to keep them out of the water and mud. Chickens and pigs were often located below. The only electricity and plumbing were in the hospital and school buildings. Toilet paper could not be flushed due to the low water pressure. I was often tasked with writing notices in three languages—Spanish, English, and Miskito—reminding people to put paper and trash in the covered waste baskets.

The laundry was a calm, rocky side stream off the river. Dirty clothing was washed by hand; pounded on the rocks until clean and then hung outside to dry. A nearby spot had a beach where the local children would play and picnic on the sand. One afternoon, I was tempted by calls to "Come on in. The water's fine." Older kids and adults were diving off a small bridge into the water. I jumped in too.

Closer to the mid-river, the broad, flat-water surface was not so calm. There was a strong current that caught me and started pulling me downstream. Before I could move toward the beach, the pull became stronger. I was suddenly sucked under the water feet first and moving fast. I hit a tree hidden under the surface. My feet were snagged but the current was still trying to drag me along. I was trapped under water and barely able to move.

I struggled realizing I was likely to stay stuck and drown. My life did not flash before me. Instead, my parents' faces popped into my mind, followed by a host of questions: How could summer-vacation fun turn so quickly into tragedy? How long would it take for people to realize I was gone? When would they find my body? Would my parents have any idea what had happened to me? I pictured them standing on the bridge, looking into the water—so sad—devastated.

The image propelled me into action. I was lying flat on my back, feet first, jammed under the tree trunk. I struggled against the rushing water and managed to sit up and reach forward. With adrenaline-fueled strength, I lifted the tree off my shins. I uncurled my freed legs, flipped forward, and shot headfirst down the river. Rolling onto my back, I managed to get my face above the surface and take a quick breath. Kicking hard and fast, I flopped onto my stomach, and began a forward crawl, reaching out with each arm, sucking in air each time I turned my head to the right.

I don't know how long I floundered toward the shore. I used my best swim techniques and fought the water every second. At some point, my struggling subsided. The water was much calmer. I put my feet down and touched the bottom without slipping. I could stand up! I slowly slogged to the river's edge. I lay down on the rocks and leaves, kissed the ground, and hugged my parents in my mental picture.

By the time I picked my way along the river's edge to rejoin the group, they were leaving.

"Hey, where were you? We saved you a soda."

All I could say was, "Thank you."

By Kimberly A. Edwards

Kimberly A. Edwards, author of 200 articles and narrative nonfiction works, and of *Sacramento Motorcycling, A Capital City Tradition* has championed writing for 40 years.

In the 1980s she founded a 12-page monthly writer's newsletter that gained mention in *Publishers Weekly.* Her credits include *Writer's Digest, International Travel News,* the *Times of India,* the *Sacramento Bee, Cosmopolitan, Seventeen, Sacramento News and Review, Food Wine and Travel Magazine,* and the *California Literature Review.* In her *Memories and Memoir Seminar,* she helped attendees turn memories into enduring stories. She has studied at the Kenyon Review Writer's Workshop and Squaw Valley of Writers.

She is the recent past president of the California Writers Club, Sacramento, and has served in various officer positions. In 2013 she received the Jack London Award for service to the club.

To contact Kim, use the address kimberlyedwards00@comcast.net.

Moroccan Vendor on a Malaga Street

Frank and I sat outside the Café Flor on a bustling Málaga street in Southern Spain. A street vendor in sandals shuffled by, swinging a plastic bag. His dark eyes and bronze skin were more Arabic than Spanish. On his forearm he carried a toy toucan. He doubled back to our table to show off the bird. When he pressed a button in the tail feathers, the bird tweeted. The exhibition was hilarious; the cutest bird I'd ever seen. But Frank waved him on, as our suitcases were already full.

Moving two tables down, the vendor stopped at a table occupied by two pale-complexioned men, tailored in cardigans, collared shirts, and plush shoes. At their ankles lay a curly-haired Maltese dog on a glittering leash. The two Spaniards, engrossed in conversation, ignored the vendor brandishing a chirping bird.

"That bird looks so real," I whispered to Frank.

I watched the vendor from the corner of my eye, lest he detect any interest and come back.

The vendor set the bird down to free an arm, allowing him to extract a model airplane from the bag on his other arm. It appeared he pushed a button on the belly of the plane, causing the body to lurch up and down as if surfing the air. The Spaniards looked up and laughed, pointing to the nose and wings rising and dipping.

One of the Spaniards took the airplane and ran his fingers along the trim from nose to tail. Every now and then our waiter passed, ignoring the vendor while grinning at diners and asking what else he could bring them.

"*Buen precio* (Good price)," said the vendor to the Spaniards, enticing them to buy. I noticed his accent was different from what we'd heard in Málaga.

"He's speaking Spanish with an Arabic accent," said Frank, a native Spanish speaker.

The two men continued inspecting the plane. "*Por favor,*" said the vendor, pleading with them to buy. The Spaniards seemed not to hear.

Soon the vendor's request stretched into a long "*Pleeeeeease,*" in Spanish.

It wasn't long before the vendor began to beg. The scene became almost painful. He all but gave away his dignity while the Spaniards ignored him.

"Call the poor man over," I muttered to Frank.

"We can't take that bird back to the States," he said.

One of the Spaniards scooted his chair away from the table, stood up and reached into a back pocket, presumably for Euros to give the vendor.

In that very moment, a dog came running from a nearby newsstand, lapping up scraps under our table. The disruption diverted my attention from any transaction between the vendor and Spaniards. But soon, elevated voices drew my interest back.

"You cheated me," said the vendor, throwing up his arms.

The Spaniards shook their heads.

"Cheats," cried the vendor. His hair was tousled, his shirt lifting over his belt.

The Spaniards dismissed the outstretched hand. It wasn't clear if they had purchased the plane, but the vendor wanted money.

"You tricked me! You tricked me!" he yelled, growing more agitated. "You need to pay the amount you said!"

Passersby, alarmed by the outburst, stopped to watch the vendor standing at the table with the Spaniards. It was hard to tell who the crowd was rooting for, but the crook in their necks suggested they were witnessing an injustice.

"The vendor's being cheated," said Frank as the waiter circled among tables, smiling, and nodding at customers, seemingly unaware of the vendor's pleas. I continued to eavesdrop while concealing my vigilance over the rising drama.

One of the Spaniards again stood up, grabbed the airplane, and led the Maltese into the restaurant. The other got up to follow his friend into the restaurant as the vendor's tirade continued.

"What can we do?" I asked, fidgeting in my chair.

"We can't interfere," said Frank. "The vendor is likely a Moroccan living here illegally. He has no rights here and the Spaniards know it."

With the two men gone from the table, the vendor stayed ranting over their plates and wrinkled napkins. A line of perspiration appeared on his shirt. Meanwhile, the Spaniard with the Maltese exited a side door, out of the vendor's view, joining a group of regulars at a high patio table.

The second Spaniard returned to pay the bill, only to find the vendor hovering at the table. "I'm waiting for my money," demanded the vendor.

The Spaniard ignored the ardent voice and extended hand. He entered the restaurant where, like his friend, he slipped out the side door to join the group of regulars.

"Look what they're doing to the vendor," said Frank. One of the qualities I like about Frank is his empathy for people unjustly treated.

When it became apparent that the men were not coming back, the vendor walked over to his motor scooter parked on the street. Every so often he looked this way, presumably to see if the men had returned.

With the stand-off ended, the crowd dispersed. The only sound was the zoom of passing motorbikes. The vendor returned with two bulging blue bags. He emptied the contents onto a table by ours: little red cars, carved wooden spoons, and several toucans, which he carefully lined up as if on display. Then he plunked himself down in an adjacent chair.

Our waiter appeared, passing our table, heading straight to the vendor whom he had previously ignored. Both men beamed. The vendor stood up to greet the waiter. They embraced and slapped each other's backs, trading updates in Arabic as if they were relatives or boyhood friends.

After a few minutes, the waiter went back into the restaurant. The vendor sat down and reclined against the stucco restaurant wall. He stretched out his legs. The server returned with a cup of espresso; his face filled with warmth for the vendor.

The vendor lit a cigarette after the waiter excused himself. He inhaled and exhaled slowly. His smoke blew over our table. He took his time sipping his coffee. He closed his eyes and rested against the wall as if he owned it. A warm Málaga breeze passed between our tables. The restaurant manager came out and told him to pick up his goods and leave. The vendor took his time to finish his cigarette and coffee. He collected his merchandise, hooked the toucan around his arm and adjusted his belt before ambling off.

"Did we miss something?" I asked when the vendor was out of sight. My head was spinning.

"We missed nothing," Frank said, the lines in his face softening. "It's the same old story. The privileged taking advantage of the vulnerable. We sat here and saw it all."

Ronald Javor

By Ronald S. Javor

Ronald Javor has written seven illustrated books for preschool and early elementary school readers about children who face hurdles involving homelessness, their abilities or disabilities, and how they overcame by way of imagination, perseverance, and the support of family and friends.

In 2020, he published *Our Forever Home*, a young adult book featuring two extinct animals, a Galapagos tortoise and dodo bird.

Ron is a retired public attorney whose professional career has involved helping build and preserve safe and affordable housing and shelters for those in need. He has volunteered for decades with local organizations serving homeless and other poor households.

His life's work has been acknowledged with several national, state, and local awards. Three of his children's books have received awards—all chronicled at ronaldjavorbooks.com.

Bingo Makes a Friend

Bingo and I were enjoying our daily jog along the river levee, sweating in the warm sun, smelling the floral aroma of spring in the air. We watched birds and insects float and zoom over and around us and heard the river lapping the shore.

Bingo is a chocolate lab-pit bull mix I rescued from the shelter six months ago. He has the large head of his pit bull parent incongruously attached to the lithe body of his lab parent. It took a while for him to become confident in open areas; he had been raised in cages and crates. He now enjoyed the vigorous open-air excursions as much as I did.

We ran, as we always did, far from the river's edge. I wasn't afraid Bingo would fall in, I was nervous about the groups of homeless people and their dogs who were unfriendly when approached by outsiders. A few would wave to us, but most ignored us or quickly disappeared in the bushes to become inconspicuous.

I mechanically loped on the trail at my fixed pace. I often wondered what life was like for them—both the humans and their dogs—and why they were homeless on the river. I never expected I might ever meet any of them or reach out to help them, but I was always conscious of warnings I received to avoid them.

We approached a wide turn on the trail and Bingo, instead of staying on the path with me, rushed off through the brush and took a shortcut. Suddenly, I heard him yelp with pain. I watched him take a couple of unsteady steps and then I watched in horror as he looked back at me and collapsed.

I immediately ran towards him, yelling "Help, help! He's hurt!" Bush branches tore my clothes and scratched my arms and legs as I went to his rescue, but I ignored them and focused only on my fallen companion.

When I got near him, I saw he was unconscious and lying in an unnatural way with his legs splayed behind him. I picked up his head, but his eyes were closed; he was completely limp. I looked back up the trail and saw a couple of other people standing there. I called out again, "Help me! Help me! He's unconscious!"

From nowhere, two strange, ragged men appeared, running from the riverbank towards us. They were large, wearing dirty t-shirts, shorts, and baseball caps. They were waving their arms at me, saying something I couldn't understand. In any other circumstance these homeless men would have scared me, but my attention was on Bingo. He still wasn't moving or breathing.

One of the men tried to kneel next to Bingo. He pushed me away to get closer to Bingo. I looked up at him as he was reaching down to the dog. He was agitated, his hands were shaking, and he had a scared look in his eyes. He didn't even look at me, but just focused on Bingo. I tried to push him away, but he pushed me back and bent in closer. I screamed for him to go away, but he only pushed me harder as he moved closer to Bingo and touched him.

"Get away, get away!" I screamed. "Leave him alone, you dirty stranger!" I shoved him again with all my might but with no effect.

"March. March," he responded with a flat tone and then nervously reached down to touch Bingo's head.

"Easy, friend," he whispered to Bingo, "What's your name, buddy?" Then he stroked Bingo's head and repeated his odd mantra, "March. March."

I tried again to move him away. This time I tugged at him from behind but he had wedged himself between me and Bingo. His shirt tore in my hand, and then his friend started pulling me away, saying, "Leave him alone, Jerry can help you and your dog if your leave him alone.

There was nothing I could do but watch.

Jerry knelt next to Bingo and repeated, "March. March. I'll help you, doggie. Just help me help you. Let's march." Then he slowly stretched Bingo's body out and turned him over on his side, feeling all parts of his body as he did so. His hands kept twitching as he seemed to be carefully studying both Bingo and the ground around him.

Now I was completely freaked out and getting angrier. "What are you doing? What do you think you doing? Can't you see he's hurt? Don't move him until we know what happened."

Jerry looked back at me for a moment, with anger and an emotion I couldn't recognize in his eyes. "I'm helping your dog. I know what to do. I've checked, it's no 'em,'we need to march ahead!"

Then he laid down next to Bingo, lifted Bingo's head, and looked in his mouth. His long fingers reached down his throat, explored under his tongue, and still further down his throat. Seconds later, he looked back at me and said, "No 'ay' either. We need to march quicker now to 'ar' to save him!"

I was completely bewildered at his actions and words, and started to object again, but before I could, his friend said to him, "Come on, Jerry! March, march, next!"

At that point, Jerry rose to his knees, picked Bingo up by his stomach and slapped his back a couple times. He shook him and then slapped his back again! "Not 'ar,' no 'ar,'" he said to me and his friend with concern. "March, march, we need to start CPR right away." He put Bingo down again, put his mouth over Bingo's mouth and snout, and slowly started to breathe into him. He did a couple breaths and then slapped Bingo's chest, repeating the process several times quickly.

After what seemed like an eternity, but was probably only a minute or so, Jerry sat back on his haunches and looked quizzically at the still inert Bingo.

"There's a problem, I've done everything right, but I can't seem to get much air into him. He must have fallen and hurt something internally. I'll look again. March always works!"

At that point, I heard a siren approaching and then stopping nearby. Moments later, two paramedics ran along the trail towards us carrying a stretcher and medical bag. I turned back to Jerry and Bingo.

I explained to Jerry that Bingo didn't fall until after his yelp of pain. Jerry looked closely at Bingo again and then reached for his chain collar and pulled on it. He looked up in surprise. "March, march, it was 'ay,' not 'ar.' Look!"

I couldn't see anything as he fumbled with the dog collar, unsnapped it, and pulled it off over Bingo's head. Then he started the CPR again and within moments Bingo started moving his legs. He gasped slightly and opened his eyes. He laid there looking up at Jerry and continued to gasp as he tried to get up.

Jerry looked at me and smiled, and then exalted said, "We saved him! March always works. His collar probably got caught on a branch when he was running, became twisted, and cut off his breathing. That's also why my CPR didn't work at first. March, march, it always works. It was 'ar' all along."

I hugged Bingo. "Don't worry, buddy, you'll be okay." I told Bingo again and again. For a few moments, the entire world had compressed to consist of just the two of us.

At that instant, the paramedics ran off the trail and arrived next to us. I could tell by their shocked looks that they were astounded their rescue involved a dog rather than a human. I just hugged Bingo and said over and over, "Thank you, thank you, you'll be okay, you'll be okay."

One paramedic knelt to ask what had happened. I looked away from Bingo and realized the two homeless men were nowhere in sight. I quickly explained what happened and what the two men had done. He immediately reached into his bag and pulled out an oxygen mask and a small cylinder. He put the mask over Bingo's face, holding it tight while Bingo breathed fresh oxygen. Within a minute or so, he was wagging his tail and trying to stand. up

I was able to sit back for a moment, take a few breaths, and begin to get over my panic. I looked around again but still didn't see Jerry and his friend. I asked why the ambulance had come, and they explained that someone made a 9-1-1 call about an injured person on the river trail.

"Can we help you to your car," the paramedics asked. I thought for a moment and then answered, "I'd appreciate it, but first I must find the two homeless men who saved Bingo's life. I must thank them for giving me his life back."

"You won't find them," he responded, "They're long gone from anywhere nearby. We know who they are from prior contacts with them. They're both Iraq War veterans, both suffer from PTSD, and Jerry was a field medic who saw a lot more human blood and gore in his six months than I'll ever see during my entire EMT career."

He continued explaining, "Towards the end of his tour, Jerry began having flashbacks and other psychological distress. He received a medical discharge. Just like your dog, he was injured. He's never has been able to get the psychiatric treatment he needs. He's been homeless here in Sacramento since he returned from the military. His family and former friends don't want to deal with him and his problems. His only friend is another veteran and they both self-medicate for their pain and memories." He added with sadness in his eyes, "It's such a shame. Jerry received several medals of valor for saving lives under fire but threw them away before he left Iraq. If anyone official, like us or a police officer or social worker, comes near, he runs away. I really respect him for what he did over there, and I wish we could find the key to getting him back on his feet."

"Well," I said, "Bingo and I are going to find him and try to help him get his life back like he did for Bingo. That's going to be my mission.

Maybe his problem is dealing with humans. Maybe I can find him an animal care job with a veterinarian or the zoo. I'll bring some food and clean clothes for whenever we come and run here. Maybe he'll let us become friends. He'll know, for sure, that Bingo loves him.

"One other question before you leave," I asked. "I don't know whether you know the answer, but I'd sure like to know. As Jerry tried to save Bingo, he kept repeating 'march, march.' Then he kept saying that 'em,' 'ay', and 'ar' didn't work. Do you know if that has something to do with Army discipline?"

"Great question. I'm glad he still remembers his medic training," the older paramedic answered. "That's probably what helped him save your dog."

"What do you mean? What does marching have to do with medical care?"

"Oh, it's not that kind of 'march,'" the paramedic laughed. 'March' for Jerry is really 'MARCH' in all capitals. It's mnemonic for the steps in field care and the order for saving a person's life. The 'M' is for 'massive hemorrhage control' to first stop bleeding. 'A' is for 'airway' to look for anything blocking breathing. After the first two steps, the 'R' is for 'respiratory management,' usually to start CPR or other breathing assistance. Jerry merely kept reminding himself about 'MARCH' as he gave your dog assistance. That's how he saved Bingo's life. Jerry didn't have to reach the last two steps in 'MARCH.' 'C,' for circulation (keeping the patient flat and warm), and 'H' for 'head injury or hypothermia.

The medics began packing up their equipment. Bingo went over to them, tail wagging, hoping to find a treat in their medical bag as he often did in my purse. We said our good-byes. I looked up and down the riverbank to see if I could spot my two new friends. No luck.

I promised the medics, myself, and Bingo during our walk to our vehicles that we'd be back soon, and that we'd try to repay the favor to Jerry, his friend, or other homeless people like them. Rather than trying to find them today and thanking them with words, I'll go home and think about what they need. Then Bingo and I can come back to thank them properly.

champion

Linda

By Linda Champion

Author of two books and district champion at Toastmaster's International, Linda Champion knows how to invite people into her book.

Linda's *Fairy Tales for Life: A Collection of Fourteen Original Short Stories* won first place in the children's books category at the 2015 San Francisco Book Festival and first place among children's books, at the 2016 Amsterdam Book Festival.

A retired high school teacher, Linda (ChampionWritingCreations.com) is a CWC Sacramento board member and she frequently presents on the subject of fairy tales,

Linda is currently working on a second book of fairy tales. She has also written a memoir called *Conversations with My Auntie Margaret about Sporty Dog*.

The Flower Garden

In the middle of Fairy Land was a beautiful flower garden. It was tended by a special fairy who knew the favorite flower of all who lived in the land. If a pixie or elf needed a gift for a friend, all he had to do was to go to the garden and ask the keeper which flower to pick.

Everyone was invited to come, except for one creature—a giant who lived in a dark cave deep inside the Great Mountains.

"He cannot come to this place of delicate blooms because of his immense size. Surely, he would trample all the pretty posies!" said the keeper of the flower garden.

What was sad was that no one had taken the time to check out this assertion. Everyone just assumed that the giant was guilty as charged, although no one had seen him even touch a flower.

A large sign was posted in front of the garden, "No giants allowed!"

This was a most unfair state of affairs. Would the giant ever have a chance to enter the lovely flower garden?

Time passed and sadly, things remained the same. All kinds of creatures, especially fairies, were welcomed at the flower garden and they were always assisted by the Flower Fairy who tended the garden.

"Now what flower is favored by the pretty pixie who lives in the glen on the other side of the Mysterious Mountain?" asked an ardent elf. "I want to please her with some of her favorite blooms," he said.

"Try the Sweet Williams. They are her favorite," said the Flower Fairy.

"Oh, I would have never guessed," exclaimed the elf.

In no time at all, the Flower Fairy had wrapped up the flowers for him. "Thank you so much," said the elf as he scampered off to the glen where his sweetheart lived.

Soon another customer appeared at the flower garden, this time a gnome, who also was looking for a flower. Again, the Flower Fairy picked the perfect flower for him. "Thank you, Flower Fairy," said the gnome. "How happy my gnome friend will be."

More days passed with the same scenario playing out over and over. Many were made happy by the giving of flowers.

But how can anyone be happy when one person is forgotten? Dear Reader, I hope you have not forgotten the giant.

Well, he was back in his cave. Did he have flowers to cheer him in his dark home? No. He was not welcome at the flower garden.

In a situation like this, it takes someone who is willing to stand up, to right a wrong. However, there didn't seem to be anyone who would. But on with the story.

The smallest creature in Fairy Land was a tiny ant. He had seen the sign that forbade the giant from entering the lovely flower garden.

One day the ant went to the garden and asked the attending fairy, "Why can't the giant enjoy the flowers, like everyone else?"

"We can't have that," replied the Flower Fairy.

"Why not?" asked the ant.

"Oh, I don't know," said the Flower Fairy, failing to remember the reason why.

"Well, since you don't know why, why don't you get rid of the rule? Shouldn't the flower garden be open to all?" asked the ant.

But the Flower Fairy would not budge. She said, "I will not give up the rule."

"I will not give up either," said the ant. So, he decided to go to the flower garden, each and every day, to ask for a flower for the giant.

"What flower would you recommend for my friend, the giant?" asked the ant the very next day.

"The giant? No flowers for him. On your way." said the Flower Fairy.

But the ant came back the next day, and again asked, "What flower for my friend, the giant?"

"No flowers for the giant," said the Flower Fairy.

"OK," said the ant, "but tomorrow I will be back again"

This became a daily routine, with the ant showing up each day at the flower garden. Always, he would be turned away with, "No flowers for the giant."

"See you tomorrow," the ant would say with surprising cheerfulness. This went on and on for a long time.

Finally, the flower Fairy realized that the ant was not going to give up. She decided to relent a bit by offering the ant a flower for his friend, the giant. The very next day, the Flower Fairy greeted the ant with, "Your friend will probably like a large bloom, like that of a chrysanthemum," said the Flower Fairy.

"No, not a chrysanthemum. It's not his favorite flower," said the ant who had visited the giant and knew the correct flower.

"How about a large, blooming rose?" suggested the Flower Fairy.

"No, that's not his favorite," said the ant. "I thought you knew everyone's favorite flower."

"But, but, but I do!" stammered the Flower Fairy.

"I don't think so."

"Is it a peony?"

"No."

"Is it a dandelion?"

"No."

"Is it a petunia?"

"No."

"Oh, rats," said the Flower Fairy.

"Oh, the giant definitely doesn't like rats," said the ant, with a mischievous look on his face. He just couldn't resist teasing the fairy.

"Well, are you going to tell me the favorite flower of the giant?" asked the Flower Fairy.

"Why yes, but on one condition," said the ant. "First you need to take down the sign that forbids giants"

Near the end of her patience, the Flower Fairy said, "Well, if you insist, I guess I will!"

"Please take down the sign now," said the ant with a smile on his face.

"OK," said the Flower Fairy and so the sign came down. From that moment on, everything changed in Fairy Land. All creatures were now allowed to visit the flower garden, even the giant. This change pleased him very much and so, he lived happily ever after.

So, what was the favorite flower of the giant? Well, I guess I should tell you before the story end. It was the Forget-Me-Not!

By Dennis Mahoney

Dennis Mahoney is the author of *Protector of the Refugee Planet*, the first in a series of novels about vigilantes seeking justice throughout the galaxy in the 30th century.

Dennis has been writing stories since the age of 6, when he composed his own comic book series on paper napkins.

Later he graduated from the University of California at Berkeley, served a hitch in the Navy, earned a law degree from the University of Santa Clara, did research and writing for a justice of the California Supreme Court, and pursued a career as an environmental attorney with the State of California.

He has received two awards from the Sacramento Friends of the Library, one for a children's picture book and one for the first chapter of a novel.

His main writing focus now is science fiction. More about his novel can be found on his website at dennismahoneystorycrafter.com.

The Price
of Freedom

C aleb plodded north, the direction of freedom. He had to keep going, resting only when he no longer had the strength to stand. The farther he got from Missouri, the safer he would be. His feet bled and his stomach rumbled. Maybe there would be food in the village up ahead. He would steal if he had to, but he would rather beg. He wouldn't go to hell for begging.

A year before Caleb's flight north, an old Indian either changed his life forever or did nothing that made any difference. He wasn't sure which.

It must have been a Sunday because Master, a Bible-reading man, allowed his slaves to worship and rest every sabbath. Caleb had already worshipped, so it was time to rest and enjoy a picnic with Sarah.

Sarah, and the Sundays he spent with her, were the only good things about life on the plantation. He'd known her for fifteen years since Master purchased him to work the fields. He and Sarah were around six when he arrived, bringing the number of slaves on the plantation to twenty. Other slaves had come and gone since then, but the total remained about the same. As Caleb and Sarah grew older the Master expected them to breed. Sarah hadn't produced any babies yet, but they were willing.

Mid-way through their lunch, an Indian rambled out of the cotton patch. He was trespassing, but that didn't stop him from sitting with the couple in the shade of an oak. His face was crinkled like a man of a hundred, but his body was straight like a boy of sixteen.

"General Jackson forced my tribe to give up our land," he told them. "Since then, I've lived apart from my people, hunting and gathering food where I can. But game is scarce and there are no crops nearby that a man can fill his belly with."

Master provided pork and plenty of bread on Sundays, so they shared. The Indian ate like a starving man, then said, "I must pay you."

Caleb and Sarah had helped him because feeding a hungry stranger was the Christian thing to do, not because they expected payment. On the other hand, if the old man wanted to reward them each with a nickel for their trouble, they weren't such fools as to refuse. But instead of money, he brought out a stone, small enough to hold in one hand and polished until it was shiny. There was a face chiseled onto one side with hollowed-out sockets that were three times the size of normal eyes, a hole in place of a nose, and a grin for a mouth. Like a skull, Caleb thought, only smaller.

"This stone can bring freedom to slaves," the Indian promised. "You have only to wish for it."

Caleb didn't believe the old man. Some of the other field hands were superstitious but not him. Magic wasn't real. Even if it were, it was too much like witchery. The Lord would disapprove.

The Indian continued, "Before you call upon the stone, I warn you. Freedom comes with a high price; one you cannot know ahead of time. You will learn this price only if you use the stone's power."

"I don't want it, Caleb," Sarah said. She shuddered. "That face gives me the willies!"

Caleb didn't have the willies, so he accepted the stone. Maybe someday he could sell it for a few pennies or trade it for something useful.

The Indian rose and took a few steps back the way he had come, then spoke for a final time.

"You have been generous, so I will give you another warning. If you ever tire of having the stone's power, do not toss it aside like so much trash. You must find someone who will take it willingly, or tragedy will fall on you."

They watched the stranger make his way back through the cotton patch. When he was a speck in the distance, Sarah grimaced. "What a wicked man. We've show him a kindness, and in return he saddles us with a rock that's full of curses."

Caleb stroked her hair in a reassuring way. "Nothing to worry about. He's either crazy or just plain lying. This rock's got no more magic in it than one of those cotton balls."

Her eyes pleaded. "All the same, Caleb. Promise me you won't throw it away."

Why not? She would feel better, and there was still the chance he could sell it or trade it someday. "I promise."

A year later, Caleb lost Sarah.

Master blamed her sale on the weevil for destroying a third of the crop. He needed cash to cover his debts. Parting from Sarah was bad enough. Knowing what the buyer would do with her was worse. She was young, fresh, and pretty, but hopeless in the kitchen. It didn't take a genius to figure out why her new owner wanted her. Master had never touched Sarah in a bad way. He said he didn't cotton to adultery and neither did the missus. But not all masters had the same morals. Or the same unforgiving wife.

The day after Sarah left, Caleb staggered in from the field flushed from July's sticky air. The field hands had begun picking cotton that morning under the stars, and the stars came out again before the quitting hour. Master had added two hours each day to their shift. The weevil's fault again; extra work to make up for crop losses.

The stone had been at the bottom of Caleb's trunk for nearly a year. He dug it out and held it in his calloused hands. It felt smooth like glass. He still didn't believe the old Indian, but where was the harm in trying? Caleb recalled the warning that freedom would come with a price. If so, what price could be worse than living as a slave for the rest of his life either trapped on the same plantation or sold into something worse? He hoped the Lord would understand. It wasn't as if Caleb was going to make a habit of witchery. One time, he vowed. No more.

He clutched the stone and whispered, "Freedom." Then because he didn't want to be piggish, he added, "For every slave on this plantation."

Caleb collapsed onto his bed. In the morning he was still a slave

Two weeks after Caleb wished on the stone, a twister attacked before dawn. The funnel swirled through the cotton field, carving a path of shattered crops, then headed for the mansion. It reduced the big house to rubble in seconds. Next, the twister took out after the overseers' cabins, slicing them into piles of lumber. But it sped by the workers as if it didn't notice they were there. In a final insult to the plantation, it smashed the fences and then spun out of sight.

Slaves poured out of their hovels and surrounded the ruins. A quick search proved what they had already guessed. Master's family was dead. Two field hands ran over from the remains of the overseers' cabins and reported the same result. Deliverance was at hand, but nobody cheered. Caleb did hear someone grumble that the overseers "had it coming."

What of the family? The two boys and a girl who on Sundays played with the slave children. Did the young ones have it coming also? Was this the price of freedom the old man had warned of? Caleb wondered. If the twister was not a coincidence, wouldn't that mean he had blood on his hands?

For once nobody was around to object if the slaves fled. If they took to the backroads, trackers might eventually set out after them. But the twister was sure to spread more chaos across the county. It would take time before anyone noticed they were missing. Odds of reaching free territory would never be better.

Master once had visitors who told of a lake so grand a person couldn't see all the way across. They came from a settlement at the edge of that lake, a town with a name that sounded like "Chick-ah-go." If it really existed and Caleb could find the way there, he could look for work.

He might have to scramble for the most menial jobs, but anything would be better than picking cotton.

If he hoarded his earnings, maybe someday he could buy Sarah.

Caleb continued his journey north through the night and the next morning without sleep. He clung to the hope that the twister's appearance was a coincidence. How could he ever be sure? If the magic was genuine, he had killed the Master's family as surely as if he'd pulled the trigger.

He was safer now that he was out of Missouri, but not yet safe enough to slacken his pace. Slave trackers had been rumored to cross into free territory, especially near the border. Every shadow on the horizon, every crackle in the bushes could be someone hunting him. Still, starvation forced him to seek help. The town ahead had a few scattered cabins. That was big enough for a general store.

At the store he waited in silence behind a middle-aged white lady wearing a dress so short it revealed a sliver of ankle. "Be with you in a minute," said the storekeeper as he piled food for cooking and cloth for sewing onto the counter.

The lady tallied her coins and gave Caleb a polite nod as she strolled through the door. It was his turn.

"Beans, please. Box of biscuits, six carrots, and as many apples . . . and bandages." He pointed to his feet. "Blisters."

The storekeeper gathered the items from their shelves. "That'll be eight and a quarter cents."

"Sir, I got no money, but maybe we can…."

"Runaway, eh? Can't say I blame you. Reckon no man ought to be forced to stick around a locality if he has a hankering to get away."

Caleb grinned for the first time since the twister struck. He might find others who believed as this storekeeper did.

"I got something to barter," he said, removing the stone from his pocket. "Kind of pretty, ain't it, if you like this sort of thing? Bet you could get fifteen cents for it."

The storekeeper examined the stone and drawled, "You got yourself a deal."

Caleb didn't know whether this man really expected to turn a profit. Maybe he was one of those abolitionist folks and agreed to the trade only because he wanted to aid a runaway. Either way, Caleb had his grub and had passed off the stone to someone who took it voluntarily. He hadn't had to beg or steal.

If the twister wasn't a coincidence, now the storekeeper had the power to free the enslaved, but at a high cost. The stone's magic, if it was for real, would probably go unused for as long as this man held it. He was a bumpkin, just a storekeeper in a third-rate town in the middle of nowhere. What opportunity would he ever have to set slaves free?

The lady had called him by name—the same as one of the great leaders of the Good Book. Moses? No. Isaiah? No.

Caleb remembered. His name was Abraham.

Rosi Hollinbeck

By Rosi Hollinbeck

Rosi writes mostly for children, but occasionally writes for adults. With a middle-grade novel, a young adult novel, and several picture book manuscripts complete, Her work has appeared in *Highlights, High Five, and Humpty Dumpty* magazines.

She writes fiction, non-fiction, and poetry. Her story-poem "The Monster Hairy Brown" was published in Thynks Publishing (London) anthology *50 Funny Poems for Children*. Several of her short pieces have won contests including second place in a recent CWC contest. She has two pieces scheduled for publication in 2018—an excerpt of her novel.

She regularly write book reviews for *San Francisco and Manhattan Book Reviews* and on her blog found at rosihollinbeckthewritestuff. blogspot.com. Rosi is also a long-term member of the Society of Children's Book Writers and Illustrators.

Peace Be to This House

I was late, and there she sat, as she sat every school day, dowager
queen of a shabby realm. Tall, stately, and stern-faced, she wore
her hair, chestnut shot with gray, in the soft, loose bun of Gibson
girls, although it was 1933. Laugh lines around her eyes had nearly
faded from disuse.

We talked about her, but none of us *knew* anything. Our parents
certainly never talked about her. Teachers were not discussed. Except by
the children and oh, how we let our imaginations run!

She lived in an old frame house. The paint, faded and chipped, was
worn by the dry, Nebraska wind. No one visited except the grocer's
delivery boy and old Doc Halbert. She never went anywhere but to
school and home. And she never kept anyone after school or in at lunch.
She rushed home at noon for an hour. At the end of each day, she
whisked away home.

Every evening a light shone in an upstairs room behind an always-
pulled, yellowing shade. On quiet summer evenings when some of us
scurried by, we heard murmuring, as if someone were quietly reading
aloud. Occasionally we heard crooning, like a lullaby. When we added
those tidbits together and divided with our prepubescent logic, we came
up with madness. The lady was obviously quite mad.

One morning, I ran all the way to school and arrived hot, sweaty,
and dusty. My hair stuck in damp strings to my forehead and cheeks. I
tried to sneak to my desk.

Miz Robertson looked up. A frown creased her forehead. The
big, round clock ticked, and Miz Robertson's pencil tapped. Her voice
broke the silence like ice cracking. "Melissa Anne. How nice of you to

join us. Would you care to share what so fascinated you, making you late?"

She *always* said that when someone was tardy. We usually made up something about a butterfly coming out of its cocoon or a flower opening at the touch of the sun Nature study went a long way with Miz Robertson.

I hadn't thought I'd be late, so I found myself with nothing but the truth. All I could think of was the time it took to replace the broken drawstring in my bloomers. I only had two pair. "One for wearing and one for the wash," Mother always said. I wasn't about to mention bloomers. I stared at the floor. My tongue stuck to the roof of my mouth like flypaper.

Miz Robertson said sharply, "Well?"

I couldn't tell the truth. But I couldn't think of a lie either. I looked at Miz Robertson and said, "No, thank you, Ma'am. Sorry I'm late."

I slid into my chair, stared at my inkwell, and waited for the world to end. A strange voice broke the silence, a soft, gentle voice. It was Miz Robertson. "Very well, Melissa Anne, but perhaps you will walk with me at lunch so we can talk."

I was in big trouble. No one defied Miz Robertson. Nobody. Boys caught throwing spit balls stood in the corner wearing the dunce cap. Girls passing notes filled the extensive blackboards with small, neat sentences. No one did anything more serious. No one, that is, until now.

I pictured myself begging to be allowed to stay in school and trying to explain where I'd learned such manners. I was used as a lesson in Sunday School, barred from the soda fountain at Myer's Drugstore, and was held up as an example of "what our youth is coming to" at town meetings.

I jumped when the noon siren went off and found myself alone with Miz Robertson. The schoolhouse had never emptied so quickly, not even on the last day. Her voice was still gentle when she spoke. "Well, Melissa Anne, would you like to bring your lunch and eat while we walk?"

A huge lump in my throat caused my voice to come out in a hoarse whisper. "No, thank you, Ma'am. I'm not hungry."

"I hope you aren't ill. Shall we go?" She moved briskly out the door. I scrambled to keep up.

In spite of the twenty-odd children in the school yard, there wasn't a sound. I don't even think birds were singing.

Miz Robertson shooed children away from the fence. "You know, my dear, I try to teach the children to be responsible, but also to use their imaginations. That's why I always ask my why-are-you-late question. It never occurred to me one of my young friends would be caught without a story. It was never my intention to embarrass anyone. I didn't realize you all took me so seriously."

We stopped in the village square, under wide, shady elms dappled with sunlight dropping between the leaves. She smiled down at me. She was almost pretty.

I wished I'd brought my lunch.

"I'm so sorry if I embarrassed you. I hope you'll forgive me." Her hand came slowly up, her fingers lifting my chin until my gaping mouth closed.

Words tumbled over one another racing to escape my mouth. I told her the tale of my bloomers and laughed when I realized how silly it sounded.

"Once my drawstring broke during Sunday School. I walked home with my elbows tight against my waist to hold them up. My arms ached for two days." Her voice was sweet and musical as she told this. We laughed. Her eyes sparkled and her face was rosy, fresh, and nearly young. When her glance fell on the clock at Rhein's Jewelry Store, her face became stone, and her laughter stopped. She turned and strode toward home.

"I must go, Melissa Anne. I'll see you after lunch." The words were tossed over her shoulder as she hurried across the square. It was the old icy-voiced Miz Robertson, as if those few minutes had never occurred. Whatever secret she had locked away in her house, it controlled her life.

• • •

My fifteenth summer, I worked for Doc Halbert. Short and a bit pudgy, wispy brown hair fast disappearing, and bags under his steady blue eyes, he looked like a saloon keeper, but he exuded confidence. I worked two hours each day doing filing and paperwork for a dollar fifty cents a week. My family was grateful for extra money because it hadn't snowed much that winter and the ground didn't look good for crops. I'd been working only two weeks when he told me someone asked if I could be hired away for seven dollars a week. With that much money I could save some for college.

"You remember Miz Robertson, don't you? Your grammar-school teacher?" I nodded. My mouth dried as memories floated in my mind.

"Well," he went on, "she suffered a slight stroke. She needs someone to help out and told me you could be trusted."

Trusted. Interesting choice of words. There was no question, though, in view of the money he'd mentioned; I would take the job.

When the last morning patient left, we locked up for lunch and left for Miz Robertson's house.

Doc walked with his head thrust forward, whistling, coattails flying, and hands jammed into his pockets. I sprinted to keep up.

When we reached her front gate, fear gripped me. I remembered the rumors we passed around as children, the madness we assumed that held this woman in its grip.

Doc strode in, stopping just in time to keep the screen door from slamming.

She sat in a wing-back chair in the formal parlor. Her back was straight as a ruler, but somehow, she looked comfortable. One side of her mouth smiled slightly. Her voice was gentle and soft as it had been that long-ago morning, just thicker and halting.

"Melissa Anne, how good to see you. I've missed you since you moved on to high school. How are you, my dear?"

Though fifteen, I became little again, my voice childlike. "Just fine, Ma'am. How are you?"

What a stupid question. My face heated up.

Her eyes softened and that half smile appeared again. "I'm quite well, thank you. I'm glad you're here to help. My right side isn't working correctly since my illness and, well, I need some assistance." She seemed to be embarrassed by this. I expect it wasn't often she asked for help. She got up slowly and turned to Doc saying, "Shall we go up, Thomas? Charles is so looking forward seeing you."

Charles! So there really was a secret, and I was to be privy to it. I suddenly wished I could go to the bathroom. But I followed along, my mind racing, unable to follow the chit-chat between Doc and Miz Robertson. They walked through a long upstairs hallway toward the room I knew must be behind that infamous yellowed shade. The mystery chilled me, and I found it hard to get a good breath.

I recalled the time Aunt-Beatrice-with-the-goiter came to visit. Mother told me her huge goiter came from swallowing chewing gum. I had just swallowed mine in the excitement of having a visitor. I felt the same way now, a sickening dread filling me.

The door swung in on well-oiled hinges. A man lay propped up by sparkling white pillows. He had sunken brown eyes, open but vacant. He had slack skin, pale and as yellow as the window shade. His neatly combed black hair was streaked with dull grey. His gnarled, bony hands lay crossed in his lap, one thumb twitching regularly.

Miz Robertson leaned over, brushing his parchment cheek with her lips and murmured, "Hello, Charles darling. Thomas is here." Though her right arm hung limply, her left hand plumped pillows and straightened covers. She took a damp cloth from a bowl on the bedside stand and washed his face and hands, talking all the while. He never spoke or moved except for that small regular twitch of his thumb.

"And we have a lovely young friend with us. Her name is Melissa Anne, and she will be helping until I'm feeling better." She turned to me. Waiting. Expectant. I stood frozen in the doorway.

"Come in, Missy." Doc reached out and took my hand, drawing me to the foot of the big four-poster. Bright chintz curtains hung inside that yellowed shade, and children's crayoned pictures covered one wall. I recognized some of the older ones.

"Afternoon, Charles." Doc chatted as if he'd met someone on the street. "Missy has been helping me at the office and I'll miss her. But you and Evey need her more, so I'll relinquish her—but just temporarily—until Evey is better." He turned to me, smiling broadly. "Say hello to Mr. Robertson, Missy."

Heavens! Miz Robertson had a nickname—Evey. All these years she hadn't even had a first name. And a husband!

They each covered his hands with theirs as they spoke. And they looked directly into those vacant, unseeing eyes. I stood at the foot of the four-poster staring just above his head. That child's voice was still with me as I whispered hello.

Doc pulled his stethoscope from his jacket pocket and did a quick exam on his patient-friend, talking as if they were at an ice-cream social. "Charles, you will never guess who stopped to see me last week. Remember Harper, that fellow who had the spread south of Shakopee? He came all the way up to see me because he didn't trust the young pup who took over my practice down there. That young doctor told Harper he had an ulcer, but Harper insisted it was a cancer, convinced he was dying. Well, he's got an ulcer, right enough, and a wasted day to go with it." Doc chuckled as he put away his stethoscope. He straightened up and spoke to Miz Robertson. "Evey, we're going down to fix lunch and will bring it up shortly."

He took my arm, led me downstairs, and sat me on a hard kitchen chair. He took a covered saucepan from the icebox and set it on the stove to warm. "Well, Missy, I guess you'd like to know what the hell is going on."

I'd never heard anyone curse except for tentative little-boy curses occasionally floating from behind the boys' outhouse at school. That got my attention.

"Charles is my best friend. He and Evey and I grew up together.

They married nearly twenty years ago. So young and in love." He shook his head sadly. "She was only to teach until their first baby. Did you know she's only thirty-nine? No, of course not. Charles had a beautiful farm, but that first autumn he had an accident during harvest. Nobody knows how long he lay hurt until Evey found him. And there isn't much we can do about that kind of head injury. We just don't know enough. Damn, it's so frustrating!"

His fist came down on the table, scaring me out of half a year's growth.

"Anyway, he's been pretty much like that," he indicated the room upstairs with a wave of his hand, "since and probably will be for a long time to come. Most likely forever."

Doc set up a tray with a glass of cold milk and scooped warm vegetable soup into a crockery bowl. He finished with a crisp white linen napkin and some worn flatware from the sideboard.

"Evey's never stopped loving him and hoping things will change. She has just gone on with her life, doing what had to be done. I admire her and respect her wish for privacy, although I will never understand it. Damn foolishness, if you ask me, that one feels ashamed for such a thing." His knuckles rested on the table and his eyes looked squarely into mine. "I hope you will respect that wish, too, Missy."

He straightened up. "I've got to get back to the office. You take this up, and I'll see you in a few days." He was gone and I was newly employed.

Mrs. Robertson slowly regained her strength through that long summer, while I came to know these two people, Charles and Evey. Sporadically Charles's eyes came alive, and he looked at his bride. She would become his bride, young and happy for those fleeting moments. Mrs. Robertson returned to teaching that fall, moving a bit slower, but otherwise her old self.

• • •

I went to college and became a teacher too. The town grew and I was hired to teach fourth through sixth grade while Evey kept the younger ones. As years passed, I occasionally heard children repeating the selfsame rumors we passed at their age. I often wished I could tell them the truth about her, but her secret will always stay with me.

Katherine
Henderson

By Katherine Henderson

Aspiring writer Katherine Henderson considers her genre to be memoir, although she has multiple short stories and a novel in the works.

Since her retirement, she has followed a writer's discipline, she says: "Writing with consistent effort."

"Because I interviewed his mother in 2005, my first cousin, Ken Neywick of Richardson, Texas, decided I should transcribe the manuscripts of our maternal grandmother, Hazel Willhite Cornellisson," says Katherine. "I did, and I distributed copies to family members."

True to her interest in memoir, she has collected old family letters, some dating back to the early 1900s. Since the letters have historical and cultural importance, she is preparing them for publication.

The Fire

I hadn't thought about the synagogue fire in a long time. It happened to Congregation Beth Israel on December 30, 1989, at about 3:00 a.m. Congregation Beth Israel was rebuilt, in the fall by the Bonneville County Historical Homes Tour, and rededicated the following October 1990. I paid Congregation Beth Israel $75 for a gold leaf on the Remembrance Tree with a quote from Genesis: "You meant it for evil, but G-d meant it for good."

The reason the fire came to my mind after five years was because I was chairing the annual synagogue picnic to be held on Sunday. The day before the picnic I had to get a key from someone on the synagogue board. I went to Helen Hake's store. She didn't have one, but she would call Dr. Fieldstein to have him bring his key for me to borrow.

While we were waiting for Dr. Fieldstein, Helen told me, "I haven't had a key since the fire. That totally devastated me. I was the first one the fire department notified, and I didn't know what to do. You know, they never did solve that arson." Then she looked me in the eye and said, "They say some hobos set the fire, but there were seven separate fires. I don't think hobos did it. Do you think hobos did it?"

I said, "No."

Dr. Fieldstein came with the key, and I went on with my day. That night I realized I still had a problem. I had borrowed the charcoal grill to grill the hot dogs for the picnic, but I had no one to build the fire. The person I had for last year's picnic promised he would beat lung cancer and be there to grill the hot dogs. That wasn't going to happen. I had no idea how to build a fire.

In desperation, I looked in a small cookbook entitled *Outdoor*

Cookery, and inside the front cover was a yellowed newspaper clipping on "How to Build Barbecue Fires." I was relieved.

It was 10:30 p.m. by this time and I knew Mitch was done with his surgery schedule. I called Chrisman Clinic and Mitch answered. I told him about my fire problem and its solution. Then the conversation turned to the synagogue fire. Mitch said, "So, did they ever find out who did it?"

And I said, "No."

Then he said, "Did the person who set the fire use gasoline, or something?"

And I said, "I don't know."

But I did know. To my knowledge, I had read everything printed in the *Post Register* about the fire, and there was no mention of an accelerant used. If one was used, only the person who set the fire would know that.

A couple of days after the picnic, I turned my attention back to the synagogue fire and what Mitch had said. I reread my journal entries of that December 1989.

I was a data collector at that time for the Bannock County Assessor's office and spent my days in the field looking at recently sold real estate properties. I spent afternoons in the office cleaning up those data elements for the multiple regression computer models. One December afternoon, the office specialist for our sales crew went out in the field with me. We stopped to see her long-time male friend, David. Later she told me, "You know, I've known David ever since high school and I can tell he really likes you. Why don't the three of us go out for pizza next week?"

I remembered we did and thought David was fun. We went to see the play, *Scrooge,* and just had fun. But I had a problem. I was still having appointments with Mitch. No problem, I thought. It's December. It's time for my annual New Year's Resolutions. So, I called Mitch and said, "Well, I can tell you really aren't ever going to marry me, so I'm not going to see you anymore and I'm going to marry someone else."

I didn't hear as much as a hang-up call from Mitch. By and by the threesome of the office specialist, David and I became a two-some of David and me. David was talking to me in vague terms about commitment.

On December 31, 1989, I got a call from my synagogue friend who said, "The shul burned last night and they're pretty sure it was arson." I remember I had this sinking feeling in the pit of my stomach. I was afraid that I knew who torched the synagogue.

That following January 1990 was an awful month for me. I was

RIF'd (reduction-in-force) and sent from real property to motor vehicles where I had started my career. The investigation of the synagogue arson was continuing. At this time, Congregation Beth Israel had no rabbi, so I talked to the rabbi of Temple Emanuel in Pocatello about my suspicions. I was on the Board of Congregation Beth Israel, so I talked to the detective in charge of the synagogue arson case. But I had no proof.

What I did have was nightmares. Whenever I entertained the thought that Mitch couldn't possibly have done it, I always had a fire nightmare. My most vivid nightmare was that of my mobile home burning completely to the ground with everything in it, and with me and my daughter Samantha escaping. We were standing on the sidewalk looking at our burned-out mobile home when Mitch walks past looking back and smiling his kind of half smile at us.

After the nightmares, I confronted Mitch about the fire. He yelled at me and called me crazy. I was in private therapy at the time and just barely off antidepressants from the deaths the previous spring of my father and grandmother. I decided I was crazy.

Lee Branco

Denise

By Denise Lee Branco

Denise Lee Branco is the award-winning author of *Horse at the Corner Post*: Our Divine Journey. She is also a contributing author to three anthologies.

In addition to being a writer, she is an inspirational speaker who continues to believe, dream, and overcome so those who meet her recognize the possibilities within them.

She is also a member of numerous literary and publishing organizations.

Dance in the Rain

We are living through what feels like a never-ending thunderstorm. When we take note of momentary silence and pop our head up in true groundhog fashion to see if normalcy has resumed, we discover that it's only a temporary reprieve. Another threat has emerged or is looming in the distance.

If you're like me, that's how you felt about 2020 and the months in 2021 with the unrelenting downpour of trials. Beginning in February of 2020, my father was admitted to the Intensive Care Unit with a 103-degree temperature, sepsis, and a whole lot of other scary concerns. He was readmitted to the hospital twice within a month for a slew of other health issues. Blessedly, he recovered. Since then, my family has experienced ups and downs, navigating through the unknown in a global pandemic.

Like many of you, we have had to adjust to a new reality. We have become students of infectious disease, innovators, caretakers, educators, and online purchasing experts. We have constructed plans for safety against a deadly virus for which there was no cure or available vaccine, to protect our families. Who knew that the start of a brand-new decade would test us in so many ways?

Even though our country's health crisis isn't over, hope is peeking through the clouds. Now is a perfect opportunity to reflect, reevaluate, and reimagine our lives: What have you done to grow during this unprecedented time? Did you challenge yourself to try a new hobby, read self-help books, attend a virtual class, or volunteer to help others? Have you strengthened your current relationship and reconnected with a person with whom you've lost touch? When you look at yourself today, have you witnessed resilience, renewed strength, and fresh determination?

The storms of life will continue to come and go. When clouds appear, you must seek happiness under dark skies. You must find hope swirling in the wind. You must be the encouraging light that strikes the heart of others and forges through the sound of thunder.

On days you don't feel like doing a quickstep or samba, try a waltz. Keep moving out of the storm as you dance in the rain.

By Dorothy Rice

Dorothy Rice, a San Francisco native, now lives in Sacramento.

At 60, following a career in environmental protection, Dorothy earned an MFA in creative writing from UC Riverside, Palm Desert. Her first book, *The Reluctant Artist: Joe Rice (1918 – 2011),* a memoir/art book about her father, was published by Shanti Arts.

She has essays and short stories in a number of literary journals, including *Brain, Child Magazine, Literary Mama, the Rumpus, Proximity, Longridge Review,* the *Tin House* blog and the *Brevity* blog.

In 2018, one of her stories was nominated for a Pushcart and she won second place in the annual Kalanithi Writing Contest for her narrative nonfiction.

Dorothy is working on her next book, a memoir about coming of age in her sixties.

My First Edible

My sister swears by edibles for whatever ails her, and just for fun: gummies, chocolates, and especially the cookies a co-worker bakes.

"One before bed and I sleep like a baby," she assures me.

"No weird dreams?"

"Not at all. And they're pretty yummy too. Like a butter cookie. Not all twiggy like the brownies from back in the day."

She's 61. I'm 65 and suffer from insomnia. For us, back in the day means the sixties, when we lived in Mill Valley, across the bay from San Francisco—the epicenter of the summer of Love; free concerts in Golden Gate Park, the pitter-patter of bongo drums and contact highs. "You'll love these," she says, handing me a zip-lock plastic baggie with six pale cookies inside. "But be careful. Maybe start with half. It's way stronger than what we used to get."

I stash the blonde cookies in my kitchen goodie drawer.

The next afternoon, I have the house to myself. It's hours until bedtime, but I'm curious about those cookies. I pluck one from the baggie and settle on the couch with the remote. Not bad. Nice crumbly texture. No weird aftertaste or green bits to pick from between my teeth. I gobble the entire cookie while scrolling Netflix.

The accented chatter of *The British Baking Show* provides a soothing soundtrack. I close my eyes. What's this? An intriguing thought, then another, and another. I stumble to my office for notebook and pen.

Back on the couch, I scribble furiously. Fast as my wizened fingers can propel the pen across the lined page. A prescient insight glimmers at the edge of consciousness. Did I just write *prescient*? God, I'm good.

What's this? A stabbing pain between the ribs. My back is seizing up. Must. Lie. Down.

I roll off the couch. I zig-zag to the bedroom with the notebook and pen clasped to my chest. Mustn't lose the prescient…thought… thing. I mound pillows. I resume mad scribbling, picking up where I left off. Which was where? Breathe. Concentrate. Something about time. How it passes and the numbers get bigger. Like mine. How we—me and time; time and me—age in tandem. At least in this dimension.

The bedside clock flashes 6:09. It would be cool if I could say I was 69 in 96, or 96 in 69, but then I would have missed out on childhood and adolescence. So maybe not so cool.

Ah, the summer of 69—the whole year actually. I was 15. I remember this one time. I lay on my bed, in my bedroom in the peak of our A-frame on a Mill Valley cul-de-sac mesmerized by the digital clock. I couldn't work out how all the numbers fit inside. In a flash, it came to me. You only needed 0 through 9! Every conceivable time combination with just 10 numerals; four flipping stacks of 0-1-2-3-4-5-6-7-8-9.

If I stared hard enough, and didn't blink, I could catch the flip, even see the fingertips of the tiny guy who hid inside the clock and made the numbers change. A skinny guy in a black full-body leotard. Faceless. Or you'd see the glint in his eyes. Were there four of them trapped in my clock? One for each stack? Furtively flipping 24/7? What if they escaped? I was alone in my bedroom at the top of the stairs with the door shut. No one to hear my muted screams.

Memories. I'd forgotten all about those little clock men. I get it all down in my trusty notebook. The clock on my bedside table now is electronic. No stacks of flipping numbers. It flashes 6:39. Whoa.

I kept a notebook in my teens too. Back then, I wrote in code. Mom was nosy, and scary. Now I'm the mom. Or I was. Was *I* nosy and scary?

I used to write in circles. Starting in the center. I'd turn the page round and round until I ran out of space and words dribbled off the edge. "Help me, I'm falling," the letters squealed, as they tumbled onto the floor and skittered from sight. I was always sure I was writing the most amazing thing ever. And maybe I was. But afterwards, my crabbed circles were indecipherable, forever lost.

No need for subterfuge now. I have no secrets to reveal or hide. I write on the lines and take extra care forming my letters.

What's this ache in my belly? Half a measly leftover salad from Panera for lunch. No fresh baguette to slather with butter. No compressed carbohydrates to fill the holes in my gastric soul. Must. Have. Sustenance.

It's slim pickings in the kitchen. No fresh bread. No stale bread. Half a box of wheat thins and my husband's Chips Ahoy cookies. He won't notice if I eat a few, then rearrange the rest.

The crackers and cookies are gone. Bedspread and sheets are littered with crumbs. How did this happen? I've eaten all my husband's cookies—again. Must destroy the evidence. But my belly is a bowling ball. I'm pinned to the bed. Eyelids heavy, so heavy. Must digest. Must sleep.

Now the bed is spinning. I'm Dorothy in the *Wizard of Oz*, only this isn't Kansas; there's no twister, and there's no cows, farmhouses, and Auntie Em in a rocking chair swirling by. Only queasy regrets. I grip handfuls of bedding and hope I don't lose the Chips Ahoy. So much for my sister and her soporific cookies. She promised I'd sleep like a baby. Bah.

I do sleep. Which I only know because the cell phone wakes me. It's her.

"Hey, hey, hey," my sister says, peppy as ever.

"I tried one of your cookies."

"And?"

"I got pretty high."

"In a good way?"

"Not really." I give her a brief recap. "That doesn't happen to you?"

"Nope. Hey, can I interest you in an evening stroll on the levee? Watch the sun set. Get those endorphins firing." She's practically humming with good cheer.

"Ah, no. I'm digesting."

I drop the phone, glance at the clock, 7:39. I pick up my trusty notebook. At least I wrote. I squint at the last page. Turn the notebook upside down. Sideways. Riffle through the previous seven pages of barely legible scrawl. Mysterious blank spaces. Strings of conjoined words that trail past the margin and off the page.

I check the bedspread and sheets for puddles of letters. Nothing. Gone.

Some things don't change.

By Lonon Smith

For more than two decades after receiving a masters of fine arts in screenwriting from the American Film Institute, Lonon Smith worked as a screenwriter and script doctor for hire in the Hollywood film industry while occasionally writing a series episode.

A screenplay based on his first novel is currently optioned for a film.

Two of his plays have been nominated for best original script by the Sacramento Area Regional Theater Association, and his open adaptation of Stevenson's *Treasure Island* won that award in 2018.

His current novel *Dirt on Fire*, set in the Stockton area, was completed in 2020 and still awaits publication.

To the Rescue

One of America's greatest songwriters was in the hospital, brought down by the virus that had come among us. It was time for me to say a long overdue thank you to John Prine for a favor he didn't know he had done.

Long ago, when a divorce caused me to no longer live with my children, I lived instead in a second-floor apartment separated from the next building by an alley. Across the way lived an older woman I didn't know, although she knew me from my late-night homecomings and too-loud music. These were the days when I made up for broken domesticity by embracing an ancestral need for wildness. The women were friendly and recreational drugs flowed across my table as a next-best-thing substitute for happiness.

My latest girlfriend had just moved on, leaving behind two red clay bowls filled with good earth and into which—perhaps as a joke—a friend planted some very illegal marijuana. The plants grew green and healthy, embracing the sunshine from my back window. They were my version of flowers—plants were ignored by me except for an occasional watering.

I learned how much the woman across the alley disliked me the morning the police knocked on my door. There were five of them, two men, two women in plain clothes, plus a uniformed officer who guarded the stairs in case I made a run for it—they had a warrant. The two women removed the two plants from the window, placed them in a garbage bag, and proceeded to search my apartment for any other sins.

Two of the men sat with me while she searched. I was my usual casual self, except for the inner turmoil going on anticipating there might be an even greater calamity—there were bigger plants they couldn't see. I faced the possibility of jail. I would disgrace my widowed mother in the eyes of her law-abiding family. Even worse, it would be one more blow to an already tenuous connection with my children.

This is where John Prine showed up to save me. The first of the two men noticed a trumpet a musician friend, Leroy, brought by in case I wanted to play it. I told the cop I use to play in a small-town high school band, and that the famous Mexican trumpet player, Rafael Méndez, once fronted a concert we gave.

This intrigued the first cop, who knew his trumpet players. We had an informed discussion about the famous players we both liked; trumpeters who weren't just Louis Armstrong and how the stuck valve on the trumpet he was holding made it hard to play something besides Reveille and Taps.

The other cop didn't care about trumpets. He cared about a song book he'd picked off the floor.

"You like John Prine?" he asked.

"I do," I said. "Paradise," I said. I was referring to the achingly painful song about the loss of beautiful land because of coal mining in Kentucky.

"Sam Stone," I said, referring to the best song about addiction I knew.

I didn't mention, "Hello in There," which Bette Midler had made famous a few years earlier—that would have been too obvious.

"How about the one about 'things being the same,'" the second cop said.

We mentioned a couple more songs. I told the cop I could play a couple on the guitar if he didn't require more than four chord changes and playing in the keys of E or A.

The second cop laughed. The three of us were getting along well when the search of the deepest recesses of my sock drawer ended and the lead female detective came over—to arrest me. The other female detective stood behind her holding the garbage bag now sealed as evidence.

"Write him up for less than an ounce," the John Prine fan said.

A silence passed. The lead cop frowned. She looked back at the woman holding enough weed to get my entire apartment building high. And, being it was the late '70s in America, there were some serious stoners among my neighbors.

I watched this gender struggle with more than a little personal interest. The first woman didn't like me. God knows what life in the way-too-macho Los Angeles County Sheriff's Department was like for her. Maybe she awoke this morning dreaming of bringing a miscreant like me to justice. I was, after all, clearly growing (with possible intent to sell) a plant that made people eat donuts in excess instead of getting drunk on Saturday night like decent Americans.

"Write him up for less than an ounce," the second guy repeated in a half whisper—the kind of whisper couples use when they don't want to fight in public.

The woman gave me a long look, possibly imagining me doing ten years in a desert prison with a roomy who would love my white ass way too much.

I tried to look respectable, which even Mother Teresa couldn't do with four cops having a non-argument about whether to arrest you or not.

Then, the lead detective took out a pad, wrote me a ticket, snapped it loose, handed it to me, and left. The woman holding the bag followed. The second cop told me—helpfully I thought—that I didn't need to grow weed when I lived a block off Sunset. If I couldn't score something up there, I wasn't trying.

An hour after the cops left, and I was still contemplating life, my friend Bob showed up with a baggie of some good stuff. I invited him in and told him how close he'd come to being my partner in crime. The two red clay bowls sat on the floor in the sunshine with only a promise they would sprout a green stalk. It seemed like a sign to dump both bowls and give them to the lady in the back apartment who'd grow flowers in them.

The Mexican trumpet story helped, but I know it was John Prine's music that tipped the scales in my favor. I wish I could have told him my story in person, to watch him have a good laugh, but my story was no longer relevant. John Prine died. He will no longer write great songs about American life. I am left to whisper thank you to the darkness and the wind. The need to listen to "Angel from Montgomery" is coming on strong on this Friday night in Covid land.

By Ann Sexton Reh

Ann Saxton Reh, a retired educator and award-winning writer, has lived in six foreign countries and many states.

Her years of adventure provide the impetus for her short story, memoir, and novel writing.

Her historical mystery series, set in the 1980s, features David Markam, a diplomat who uses his skills to thwart killers in exotic places. He's challenged by worldly expats on the Mendocino coast of California in Meditating Murder.

In *See the Desert and Die*, his career and his heart are at risk in Arabia. She keeps readers up-to-date at www.annsaxtonreh.com.

My Flies

The pet parade is tomorrow, and all the other kids have a pet," my son wailed.

I sighed and put down my pen. It was not the first time the pet issue surfaced. We were gypsies. Our work kept us moving and short-term landlords seldom allowed pets. But in this shiny South Bay suburb that I thought would be an ideal place to raise a family, our humiliation was about to go public.

Inwardly, I cursed whoever had the bright idea of parading animals through the streets of the neighborhood. Outwardly, I began problem solving.

"Can you take a stuffed pet? How about that dog you got from your grandmother? It almost looks real."

My son glared. "They would laugh at me. That's a baby toy."

"How about taping a wire to a leash and walking an invisible pet?"

"No. It has to be a real pet. You promised I could have a real pet when we moved into this house." He was sitting on the floor, and when I looked down at his sweaty hair, his shoulders hunched in frustration, guilt made me giddy. "Too bad we can't catch a squirrel."

He tensed and then looked up, his eyes shining. "My ant farm! I could take that!"

Rummaging through the garage, we unearthed the sleek, split-level Ant's Delight. When we ordered it last year, it arrived with a tube of large, shiny black ants that were supposed to cohabitate and multiply in their luxury home. The ants, however, arrived pre-deceased.

Now, the glamorous green plastic estate might be the solution to our problem. If we could find new residents.

Mason jars in hand, we inched along the sidewalk, searching.

After an hour, it became obvious that the neighborhood was zoned only for ants too small or too suburbanized to deign to live in a "farm."

I sat down on the curb, my son behind me pushing clumps of dirt in a flowerbed with his toe. Suddenly, he jumped up. "Worms," he shouted. "I could make a *worm* farm."

The idea of grubbing in the dirt for worms didn't appeal to me. I have a pact with things like bugs and worms. They stay in their homes. I stay in mine. Now, it appeared we were about to compromise.

Fortunately, we did find earthworms that agreed to live in an ant farm for a day, and my son went happily to the parade. I watched from the sidewalk, ignoring incredulous stares from the other parents when, among cuddly cats and perky dogs, my son passed proudly holding his worm farm.

When we moved to another house, the management did allow pets, but the security deposit—first and last month's rent—and other expenses left our budget too lean to pay the $500 pet deposit.

We lived in the new house only a few weeks when we began to hear the tap of clawed feet in the attic crawl space. An exterminator eliminated the rats for us, and I tried to forget they'd been there.

But by this time, my daughter began to feel the deprivation of being pet-less in suburbia.

"We were talking about pets in school," she told me one day.

I prepared myself for the usual heart-wrenching scene, but she didn't seem upset at all.

"The teacher wrote categories on the board: cats, dogs, birds, fish, and other."

"I'm sorry you had to say you don't have a pet," I said.

She shrugged and opened the refrigerator. "No, one other kid and I are in the 'other' list. I said mine are rats."

"Rats?"

"Well, they *did* live in the house with us."

Visions of the 'worm farm' debacle rose before me. Now, I'd be the mother who let her kids play with rats. I could only hope the teacher would assume our "pets" were the white, cute kind that live in cages and hardly stink at all.

But the issue was far from closed. A few weeks later my daughter came home with an assignment for Open House Night at school: "Make a poster about your pets."

"Mine is about my flies," she told me.

"Flies?"

"Yes, my fly collection. Would you like to see them?"

I bit my tongue when she showed me her exhibit for school. On a long strip of Scotch tape, she'd stuck the carcasses of twenty-three houseflies. Next to them was an anatomically correct drawing of a fly and a text that read:

My Flies
These are my flies.
I found them all behind our couch.
The picture window attracts them.
We try to clean them out,
but there are just too many flies.

"My goodness. How interesting," I said. Deeply instilled precepts began to surface. My own mother, I am sure, would not have let me out of the house with a collection of flies from behind the couch. But I was trying hard to encourage my children's creativity and resourcefulness. Be grateful we don't have roaches, I told myself.

The flies went to school, and I slunk through the classroom during Open House, avoiding the teacher's suspicious glances.

This was really the last straw. When someone brought a box of cute kittens to school at the end of the term, I raised the money for the deposit, and we took home a real pet.

I won't say we were entirely normal afterwards, but my kids grew up to be wonderfully resourceful. And there was even a bonus: Once we had a cat, we never again found a fly behind the couch.

Frances Kakugawa

By Frances Kakugawa

Frances H. Kakugawa grew up speaking Pidgin in Hawaii. At age six, she discovered that Dick, Jane and Sally from her readers didn't speak as she did. Fascinated, she decided then to become a writer. She protected this dream by avoiding writing courses in college, afraid a professor would tell her she couldn't write. Her collection of childhood poems was lost when her village was destroyed by lava flows.

Her first of 14 books, *Sand Grains*, a book of poems, was published when she was in her 30s. When she became a caregiver for her mother who had Alzheimer's, it was poetry writing that transformed her experiences into an art form.

She published three books for adults and one for children on care-giving. Her four award-winning illustrated children's books about a little mouse poet give children the power for change through poetry.

Today Frances is internationally published; she goes nationwide to give lectures and workshops.

Meet her at www.francesk.org.

The Eastern Way

The old Buddhist priest offered me hot green tea before explaining why he had invited me halfway across the Big Island to meet him. The room was sparsely furnished with a wooden table and two wooden chairs. I felt the chair beneath me as I tried to become a Japanese of his generation, sipping tea by holding the tiny teacup with both hands and bowing to suggest humility and gratitude. Between us lay my book of poems, *Sand Grains.*

I'd been living with both feet slightly off the ground since its publication, my first published book of poems. A six-year dream, a final reality. The Honolulu Advertiser devoted a page to its review. A bouquet of spring flowers from the mayor's office greeted me at the book signing. They called me poet. The blurb on the jacket cover read: *"Here is a pervading sense of the essential aloneness of the human spirit, the core of being hidden behind a protective mask."* The poems were written as an alternative to driving into a tree after the end of a first-love relationship with Robert. Poem after poem examined the imperfection of men, the unfairness of life, my brokenness. I was young. I was searching for the woman I was to become. Why would any of that interest a Buddhist priest? Unless he wanted his book autographed?

Except for the sound of a near-by waterfall, the room was quiet. The old priest poured me a second cup of tea. I felt it settle in my stomach and spread through the rest of my body. He sat there carefully turning pages of my book, pausing now and then. I kept turning the teacup in my hands, waiting. Finally, in halting English, he said,

"Kakugawa-san, there is much pain in your life. Permit me to explain the difference between Western love and Eastern love. In

Western love, when someone no longer loves you, you are taught to say, 'I must stop loving him since he doesn't love me back.' In Eastern love, we say, 'I will continue to love him whether he loves me or not."

After a long pause, he added, "Listen to the sound of the water, Kakugawa-san. Listen, and learn to flow with it. Learn to love and live the Eastern way."

I walked away with undefinable joy. I wanted to weep for no reason at all. I wanted to embrace the entire world. Yes. I felt such freedom. Such power. I felt a huge burden of pain being lifted out of my body. I felt strong and wise. Yes, I'd follow the Eastern way. I'd follow the flow of the river. I will let go the romantic notion of happily ever after found in novels and live life as it is. I will not be paralyzed any more.

I rushed home to write a letter to Robert. I wished him a happy life, thanked him for

all the deep emotions I discovered I was capable of feeling. I felt magnanimously wise, perhaps even wiser than he. I was young. My heart would be broken many more times. "When I am dead," I arrogantly said, "write this on my tombstone: She lived."

Three more poetry books followed the next three years. My pen anchored me, kept me attached to the worst and best of times. I was a poet, fearless, I thought, and a far cry from the poems the Buddhist priest had read.

My poetry reflected the transformation which came slowly and steadily. The process was not as easily done as these poetry lines reveal:

> "...*my hungry heart beats,*
>   *alone...like little grey wrens*
>   *crying to be fed...*"

> "...*she blooms, then clings*
>   *till shriveled veins*
>   *slowly burn*
>   *her clutching hands...*"

> "...*forgive the truth I offered you*
>   *when I said I love you.*
>   *I love you...*"

> "*Do little fallen sparrows*
>   *damningly, painfully cry*
>   *of short-lived flights*

over silver foiled lakes
and crayoned fields;

Or do little fallen sparrows
happily, gratefully whisper
I flew —
as dusk slowly turns its head
and dry dead leaves
lightly touch their statued backs?

For twenty-eight years I floated buoyantly on the come-and-go river of love the old priest had shown me. Whatever pain and grief accompanied love, above everything else, there remained the poet, the essence of what I perceived my life to be. Then I hit a rock.

Fear, anxiety, and feelings of helplessness swirled around me like the eye of a hurricane. My mother had been diagnosed with Alzheimer's. I began to drown, loaded down with heavy gear, unable to swim this river that had become such a friend to me. I was barely treading water. How do I stop Alzheimer's? How do I stop this thief from invading my mother's life? How do I capture this thief who was leaving undecipherable chalk dust on my mother's brain? I found myself in a dry riverbed.

One otherwise, ordinary day, a norm for bottomless pits, found me stuck in traffic, driving my mother from her doctor's appointment, and answering her repeated question, "Where are we going?"

"*Okasan*," I groaned. "I don't know." She must have known it was time for silence because soon the only sounds were from the radio and impatient drivers tooting their horns. We sat in silence, waiting for traffic to move.

In our silence, the Buddhist priest appeared. Soon the sound of traffic was splashing on the rocks beneath a waterfall. The aroma of green tea filled the car. Flow with the river. Flow with the river. A horn honked; the light turned green. I took hold of the oar, drove off the next ramp and said, "*Okasan*, let's go get some tea and dessert."

From then on, whenever an obstruction appeared, I embraced it. Whatever Alzheimer's stole, we lived without. Whatever time was taken, a few minutes were retrieved to sip tea and watch steam from the cup dissipate into the thin air. With my mother at my side, I listened to the sound of water and flowed to the end of our separate journeys with love, compassion, and dignity, because in the East, water flows without obstruction.

By Pete Cruz

Pete Cruz is a non-fiction writer and speaker. He is currently working on his memoir, a story of redemption titled, *Angry Eyes, My Path to Forgiveness.*

His published works include short stories in the 2015 and 2016 *Inspire* anthologies (www.InspireWriters.org). For the 2017 anthology, *Inspire: Love*, he functioned as assistant editor. His devotional piece, *Do Not Worry*, is under consideration for *The Upper Room* (www.upperroom.org), a global online ministry.

In August 2018, he was the featured speaker at the Men's Huddle, a monthly breakfast gathering at Creekside Church in Elk Grove. He hosts a weekly Shut Up and Write (www.meetup.com/shutupandwritesacto) writing session in Elk Grove.

One of his essays took second in place in the 2017 CWC writing contest, and he served as a panelist for the 2017 California Writers Week creative nonfiction panel.

My Life Spared

Twigs, leaves, and rocks pressed against my helmet's cracked face shield. I lay face-down, my vision filled with a macro view of the ground.

I rolled onto my back and unclasped my chin strap. I needed fresh air to gain my bearings. My last conscious memory was of my rear tire snaking side-to-side as my motorcycle hurtled off the road. Apprehension held me in place, fearing I could be seriously hurt.

A whisper of wind wafted through the pines. Late afternoon sun hung in a cloudless sky. No one around. I reclined on an embankment to the side of the road.

Who parked my bike? In front of me, not more than two feet away, my prized one-hundredth Anniversary Harley-Davidson Fatboy rested against a wooden mileage-marker post. My motorcycle's handlebars drooped while brake fluid dripped onto the engine. The gas tank looked sledgehammered. The windshield and mirrors were sheared free. My seat and backrest torn apart.

"You alright?" I heard Tucker shout. He had ridden his bike behind me.

"I'm okay, I think."

"Looks like your hand's bleeding."

I raised my right hand. Blood oozed from my pinkie.

"What happened?" I asked.

"You and your bike somersaulted twice in the air," he said, moving his hands in circular motion.

"Was I on it?"

"No, you weren't."

"Why is my bike sitting here like this? Did you park it?"

"No, it came down like that and stopped," he replied, shaking his head. "The bike should've landed on you. Or you should've landed on it."

The thought of being crushed by eight hundred pounds of searing hot machine made me gasp.

"Big John was behind us. He went for help," Tucker continued. "There's no cell service here."

We'd driven through the twists and turns of the mountain highway in the El Dorado National Forest 5,000 feet elevation north of Sacramento.

Minutes later, a green U.S. Department of Forestry truck parked to the side of my bike.

"I'm Dan," the ranger said, walking toward me. "Paramedics are on their way." He bent over; his face filled my sight.

"What's your name?" he said.

"Pete."

"What day is it?"

"Friday."

"Do you know the date?"

"The thirteenth."

"Friday, the thirteenth?" He raised an eyebrow.

"Just my luck," I said.

The other four in our riding group who had driven ahead of me arrived at the scene. They hadn't noticed until further down the road that I no longer followed. Grim expressions covered their faces.

An ambulance stopped and two paramedics hopped from the back and hurried to me. One of them, Kari, hovered, making quick assessments. Her calm but concerned manner settled me.

"Any pain?" she asked.

"No, but my hand's messed up."

"You think it's broken?"

"Yeah."

"Anywhere else?"

"My chest."

Jason, the other EMT, sliced my shirt open to reveal a small purple blotch. Before losing consciousness, I had used in my right arm to cover my heart, fearing I might be headed for a ravine. My hand absorbed the impact when I landed.

The rapid sound of rotating blades diverted my attention. Hovering in the clear blue sky, a red helicopter posed like a hummingbird inspecting a flower.

"Anytime there's a motorcycle crash, helicopters are sent out automatically," Jason said, noting my gaze.

Pulling her shoulder radio to her lips, Kari said to the copter, "We'll take him. His vital signs are okay. He knows his name and knows where he is. We're going to Marshall Hospital."

They secured me inside the ambulance.

Kari advised, "We're closer to Auburn, but Marshall in Placerville is the major trauma center in this area. We're 45 minutes away."

The ambulance wound through the hills. I saw through the back window our group's ride-captain, Rafael, following on his Honda Goldwing. The siren was silent. The ride seemed more for comfort, rather than urgency. Each paramedic kept a watchful eye. Jason periodically checked my blood pressure.

The hospital's emergency staff called twice for updates.

On the third update, Kari told them, "He's looking at me. In fact, we're having a nice little conversation."

I peered at her curiously.

"They're concerned. Believe me, they've seen a lot worse than you from a motorcycle crash."

We arrived at the hospital in no time at all. "Where were you going?" a young ER physician asked while the staff pushed my gurney through the corridor.

"We were on our way to a church retreat," I answered.

"I see. A bunch of outlaws up to no good," he said grinning.

"Yeah, you bikers and skiers keep us in business," a nurse added.

The hospital staff was kind and professional. They took x-rays, other readings, and cleaned me up. A short time later, the doctor stepped into my room.

"I have the results of your x-rays." His face gave no indication of my status. "You don't have any broken bones." He reviewed his clipboard and then pressed his finger to his temple. "I think I'm going to look at them again, a little closer."

He marched out the door.

Other visitors included a social worker, and a CHP officer who was instructed to wait his turn by a nurse.

The doctor soon reappeared. "I didn't find any fractures." His half-smile expressed satisfaction. "There are no indications of internal trauma. I'm going to discharge you. From what I hear, you are a very lucky man. Must be that church gang you ride with."

• • •

A church brother, Phil, arrived Sunday afternoon with groceries. I sprawled on my couch, my body dealing with the pain that happens after an initial shock wears off.

"Pastor Mark said you'd been in an accident. He didn't tell us until the evening service. There were no details. Cell phones don't work very well up at the retreat."

I pictured the pastor making the announcement in the venue's small, theater-like facility.

"I gotta tell you," Phil said, "there were 189 guys praying for you. Some of them were in serious prayer. It was really something."

"Wow," was all I could say. I normally feel humbled when one person prays for me, but 189?

"Big John arrived at our cabin around eleven o'clock. He said you were airborne and landed face-first on a tree stump. He told us, 'Pete should not have survived.'"

I pointed out my banged-up, dirt-strewn, full-face helmet on the counter. It was a memento of a ride gone wrong.

"I've been riding for forty years, and have always worn a half-helmet with sunglasses," I said, tracing my finger along my forehead. "I only bought that helmet a few weeks ago and hadn't used it on a ride until that morning. I think the Lord impressed upon me to wear it."

"The damage to your face…." Dread came over Phil's face and his voice trailed off.

I looked away and considered the grave consequences of what would've happened if I'd used my usual head gear.

"Big John said when they pulled your bike away from the post, the post crumpled. He said that's when he knew it was a miracle."

After months of physical therapy to treat my hand and muscle soreness, I was the same as I ever was. May thirteenth neared, I reminded myself of the day my life was spared. I was grateful, but I still wondered.

I heard the usual from people: "It's not your time yet," and "He still has plans for you."

"Why, Lord, did you spare me?" I asked.

His answer eluded me. There was no still, small voice. No human or supernatural messenger. No Bible verse, radio/TV or print media offering revelation. Nothing.

Nonetheless, I awaken each morning roused by daybreak filtering through drawn blinds.

God's answer is as plain as day. Each morning He says: *The breath of life is My gift to you. A new day beckons. Rejoice.*

By Barbara Jodry

The late Barbara Jodry, a Northern California resident, was a writer, editor, and retired teacher.

Her writing genres were memoir, personal vignettes, travel, and poetry.

Her short stories and poems had been published in several anthologies, and her feature articles had been published in the *Suttertown News, Peaceworks, Because People Matter,* and in the Yesteryear column in *Senior Spectrum.* Her work also appeared in *Solar Cooker Review* and *Yankee Magazine.*

Howard's Faith

When I think of my brother Howard, I see a kind, gentle man with a quiet sense of humor. I see a courageous man whose firm unswerving faith carried him through several major surgeries for cancer over a period of 30 years. Each time he faced the Big C, he'd say, "Don't worry about me. I'm gonna lick this." After each course of radiation his hair fell out, then grew back in a different color.

Now that he's gone, our childhood together seems more vivid and poignant. We were close in age and shared a childhood that excluded our siblings—who were either much older or much younger.

In the crowded old farmhouse where our family lived, Howard and I shared a bedroom until he was eight and I turned eleven. On opposite sides of the room, we slept in old-fashioned iron bedsteads. Electricity hadn't been installed upstairs yet. I was the big sister, but I was the one afraid of the dark, he wasn't. We shared a flashlight to keep the ghosts and monsters at bay. Once, he locked me in the closet. A prank? Not to me. I threw my weight at the door until it broke off the hinges. Mother scolded me, not Howard. But later I forgave him.

When my eldest brother moved to his own place, Mother decided it was time for us to each have our own room. Neither of us wanted to leave the sunny southwest corner room we had shared since Howard was a toddler. I convinced him that the north bedroom across the hall had a better view of the trains that passed our house after we were in bed. The big headlight on the steam locomotive cast a bright light on the wall as the train chugged along the line. I showed him how to kneel on top of the covers and create animal silhouettes on the wall with his hands and arms. Howard was persuaded, but he also demanded new wallpaper—with airplanes on it.

When Dad decided Howard was old enough for some regular chores, he took him to the cornfield to introduce him to the fine art of hoeing. After showing him how to loosen the soil around the corn plant and remove the weeds, Dad left. He expected several rows to be finished before the noon break for dinner.

I can testify from experience that nothing is more lonesome for a nine-year-old than being alone in a five-acre cornfield on a hot June morning. The air heats up and the dust from hoeing rises into your nostrils. I peeked out the upstairs window and saw my forlorn little brother dallying along the row, half-heartedly whacking at weeds, stopping often to rest. I felt so sorry for him. I wanted to go out and help, but Mother had other tasks for me. Later, when I went outside to hang laundry, I heard my little brother in the field. Howard was singing as he worked. He was singing, "Don't Fence Me In."

Howard's most formidable challenge appeared when he entered first grade. By second grade, it was clear he was not learning to read. No one knew what to do. In those days, learning disabilities sometimes ended up folded into that sad old label, "retarded." Howard definitely was not mentally deficient. He had no trouble handling the paper route of the 60 customers passed down from sibling to sibling in our family for years. Mother consulted teachers and doctors. Clinical testing showed his brain could not tell the difference between various letters of the alphabet and he often reversed syllables in conversation. We now have a term for what he experienced: severe dyslexia. He never completed public school.

When the Korean War started, he was drafted and sent, not to Korea, but to Germany. The U.S. Army did not care whether he could read or not. Two years later he returned home with a Bavarian cuckoo clock for Mother and marksmanship medals for himself. Honorably discharged, he went to work in a local factory, but poor reading and writing skills kept him in low-paying jobs for most of his life.

Later, he told me how he met and wooed Kitty, his wife of 42 years. He took her son John fishing and camping to persuade both that he'd be a great husband and father. It worked. He legally adopted John shortly after their marriage.

Then came the cancer that hounded him for 30 years. First on the neck, then in a leg, then the spleen, finally, the lungs. Several years passed between each episode. The surgeries and radiation took a toll. His physician once told me, "Your brother is the most courageous patient I've ever had. No whining. No demands. He accepts the inevitable. He wakes up each morning thankful for one more day at life. He has the kind of faith and determination that keeps men alive." Over the years, his courage inspired other cancer patients.

Shortly after his seventieth birthday, time ran out. There was one last cancer, and he was gone. At the memorial service, a woman who was attending made her way through the mourners to meet me. She was Howard's tutor. She'd been working with Howard for the past six years. She said he was reading quite well, but writing continued to be a hurdle. She told me he never achieved his ultimate goal: to write a love letter to his wife. But he never stopped the lessons, hoping he would be able to before he was gone. His determination to master his learning disability inspired his teacher to remind her clients, "If a 70-year-old man will keep working to conquer dyslexia, you can, too."

Howard knew two of life's big secrets: HAVE FAITH and NEVER GIVE UP. It earned him 30 additional years of happiness.

By Kathy Lynne Marshall

Kathy "Kanika" Marshall wrote *The Ancestors Are Smiling!,* a collection of uplifting, funny, touching, maddening, and sometimes harrowing real life stories, creatively told by Marshall's ancestors and their descendants.

In 2018, she published a research-oriented storybook investigating her enslaved ancestors from Maryland, titled *Finding Otho: the Search for Our Enslaved Williams Ancestors.* These true stories are woven by Marshall with the African fabric of American historical events. Marshall has been exploring her family roots off and on since 1976 and is a self-avowed missionary for family history.

Marshall was a researcher, analyst, and technical writer for the California Highway Patrol for 36 years. In addition, she has been the owner/artist for her Kanika African Sculptures business since 1993, sharing her love for African fabric, clay, welding, and ethnic-inspired, indoor-outdoor sculptures.

It's Story Time

Hush up now," I said, watching my grandchildren making a ruckus on the porch. They were laughing, jumping, and running back and forth in a rowdy game of tag. It was twilight on the first sweltering summer evening of the twentieth century. The Barnesville Gas and Electric Light Company began installing streetlamps in 1895. Unfortunately, that improvement didn't reach our colored section of town. Instead, oil lanterns and lightning bugs brightened the dark corners of my small yard. The children squealed like piglets while catching the glowing fairies which tickled their little palms.

Everyone gathered in my yard to pay attention to *me*, their beloved elder, Margaret Booker. The spirits of my father and stepmother, Edward, and Eve Backus, floated nearby, transparent to all but me. Three of my grown sons sat in rickety rockers smoking pipes like old men after a hard day's work. Three of my grown granddaughters sat like glamour queens on the other side of me.

Granddaughter Ida was her usual prim and proper self, sitting quietly at the edge of the stoop, her hands in the lap of her homemade dress from flour sacks, watching the younger children settling themselves on the grass.

We had a big crowd tonight. My feet began tapping a rhythm beneath the patchwork skirt I had designed from discarded clothes. Excitement building, I lowered my bulk into an antique rocking-chair next to the front door of my gray, clapboard house. It had been renovated from a crude log cabin some years ago.

What a stylish family. My eldest son, Joseph Booker, had created. He was obviously doing very well in Mount Vernon, Ohio. He was the only colored machinist hired at the Cooper Bessemer Corporation there. You see, old Massa's spinster sister had taught him to read during slavery when it was illegal to do so. Being able to read and write got his foot into the door, but Joseph's dedicated work habits helped him get a good job building engines. Usually, Negroes were only offered janitorial jobs at Coopers.

Oh, that Herbert! I have never seen a boy dressed in such fancy clothes. Joseph's ten-year-old son looked like a little soldier doll. And would you look at the amazing hat on granddaughter Ada Mae's head. Seemed like it had a life of its own; was it knitted, or was that a fluffy brown rabbit on her crown? All my granddaughters have such lovely locks—Massa John Earle doubtless had some input on the shininess of their hair.

"You got a fine family there, Miss Margaret," my pale next-door neighbor called out.

"Mighty fine," added deep-voiced Mr. Patterson from across the street, still in his black coveralls the same color as his skin.

"Ev'ning, y'all." I waved at my neighbors who were watching us intently. Their observations brought the biggest smile to my lips. As fine as my family looked, you better believe I'd be the subject of gossip for many weeks to come.

"Ida Mae, bring me a cool glass of sweet tea, would ya, hun, in case I get choked up talking about the old days."

"Okay, Grandma," Ida Mae's sweet voice replied as she jumped up, smoothed down her dress, then bounded through the screen door into the narrow house. The front room crowded with furniture led into the yellow kitchen. A massive table overwhelmed the space; its chairs currently being used outside. Waiting for her return, I cooled myself with a stiff paper fan from the Captina African Methodist Episcopal Church. It had a blond Jesus holding a white lamb printed on the front, while the church's name graced the back.

"Thank you, darlin'." One sip of the sweetened blackberry tea was all I needed to clear my throat. Once everyone quieted, I began tonight's show.

I asked my audience, "So what kinds of stories do you want to hear tonight? Do you want to learn about the man who bragged he was 'The Indian Killer'?" The boys and men all shouted and waved their arms in the air, affirming their choice.

"Would you like stories about the Civil War battles in my backyard?" The same males cheered.

"How about when Ole Black Jerry ran away from his master?" The younger kids shrugged their shoulders probably not knowing what that meant, but the men once again shouted, "Yes!"

"What about the true story of being sold for one dollar?" The adults looked a bit uneasy, fidgeting in their seats, while the children remained quiet.

"How about when I fell in love for the first time?" The women and girls all gushed and sighed.

"How about when we slept under the stars on our escape here to Barnesville?" Everybody clapped and cheered at that choice.

"Well, tonight, I think I'll start with myself." In a steady school-teacher voice, I began my tale.

"For nigh onto forty years, since mid-1863, I've lived right here on Vine Street. Us old codgers like to sit on the porch in our comfy chairs, just like tonight, sharing a brief look at the past with our beloved families and friends. Our present is usually much better than our past, making us feel like we're progressing as a race.

"Now, you may not believe this, but when I look in the mirror, I see my granddaughter, Myrtle Lavata Booker, looking right back at me."

One of the kids sniggered, not believing that a sixty-five-year-old woman with some wrinkles here and there, thought I looked anything like the gorgeous lady sitting next to me. What a beauty. She wore a white dress with a deep-green, diagonal lattice pattern on the bodice, her barely tanned neck completely covered with dainty white lace. Her posture was erect, like that of a graceful ballerina. Hard to believe she was the product of my loins, one generation removed. The young'uns were still laughing as they glanced from the fashionable woman called Myrtle to me in my homespun finery.

I assured them I was serious. "No, really, she's the spittin' image of me when I was twenty. Look, we both have a Cupid's bow mouth. See how it's indented in the middle of our top lip?" I touched the indentation with my index finger.

"We both have a full bosom." I cupped my saggy breasts that had drooped to my rounded belly. All the children and men howled. The women sighed, understanding the ravages of age.

"We both have shapely hips." Myrtle and I stood up and slid our hands down our sides.

"And look at our smooth skin." I caressed my cheek with my right hand and Myrtle's with my left. "Okay, I'll admit that I may have a few more wisdom spots on my skin than she has." Everyone was laughing now, grabbing their tummies, tears streaming down their faces. They thought their grandma done lost her cotton-pickin' mind.

I sighed at the memory of youth, when I was a desirable woman with long, thick hair, and perfectly smooth, chocolate-brown skin. With a faraway look in my tired eyes, I continued speaking, almost to myself. "I was so young and pretty back then." After a long pause, a shadow passed over my eyes. "My master thought so too. You see, I was almost thirty years a slave, and I was Massa's favorite." I looked down at my hands, deep in thought.

"What's a slave, Grandma?" My four-year-old granddaughter, Anna, brought me out of my doldrums and back to the present. I gazed at her chubby-cheeked face, so innocent and trusting. How much of the ugliness and pain of being owned by someone else should I tell her? Maybe I should only talk about the happy, nice, good memories during our story time together; like the day I looked into the eyes of my first baby boy or set foot on the free soil of Ohio. No, they needed to know it all, even the time I was beaten bloody right after giving birth. Should I show them the tree of welts on my back? Wait a minute, old gal, I must be careful in how I share my stories. Truth is truth, but I don't have to tell all the details every time.

Clearing my throat again, I began speaking to my audience, empha- sizing each word. I hoped to create the sense that they were about to hear a mystery revealed, important secrets to be shared, and something special to tell their children's children when they grow old like me.

I looked closely at young Anna who had posed that simple ques- tion. Clacking my tongue, trying to find the rights words I finally said, "Honey, the answer to your question isn't easy to explain. I'll tell you 'bout my life little by little, and maybe you'll begin to understand how most black folk lived prior to the end of slavery—which was only thir- ty-five years ago." I readjusted myself, drank another sip or two of tea, then began tonight's story in earnest.

"Once upon a time in Ole Virginny...."

"'Where did the time go?' I often ask myself. It seems like only yes- terday when I was learning how to run like you little buggers"—pointing at my youngest grandchildren rolling around on the grass. "But it was actually over sixty years ago. I was born in 1834 near a small town called Beverly, located in Randolph County, in what is now West Virginny. There were fewer than two hundred people living in the entire town, and that included sixteen slaves and two free black people."

"There were a coupla boys I grew up with named George and Hugh."

I noticed the eyebrows on my sons raised in surprise; they were also named George and Hugh.

"Oh, the fun those boys and I had when we were little. Even though they were a few years older than me, we were thick as thieves. We climbed the branches of the golden poplar and oak trees near our house. We picked tart-green apples in the fall. We played tag every day around Massa's house. We tapped a stick on a metal pail to make music and made-up songs to go with it. We chased squirrels and whistled like birds. We found tadpoles and caught fish in the river. We whoop-whoop-whooped like Indians and pretended to shoot arrows at the white people who took us away from our blood families. Lying on a carpet of leaves, looking up at the bluer than blue summer sky, we dreamed of being free one day—free to live wherever we wanted and do whatever our hearts desired."

I stared into space. "Ah, nothing feeds the soul like a walk in the woods during the late autumn when a stiff breeze floats down leaves like butterflies. There's a crisp crunch underfoot, the sound of swaying branches, and the woodsy smell of pine before the snows fall." My mind floated back to that pleasurable era. A silly girlish grin appeared on my face when I remembered the first time George, Hugh and I played *doctor*.

My grandson Herbert asked, "Did you get to fool around all day long?" The question jerked me back to my audience. Could they read my mind about playing doctor?

In a serious voice, I responded, "We had chores, like feeding and cleaning up after the chickens and bringing the eggs into the log cabin so our Mistress could fix breakfast. We slopped the pigs and sometimes brushed the horses at the end of their long workday. We helped pull weeds in the kitchen garden before I was old enough to do the cooking myself.

"What kind of garden?" someone in the crowd asked.

"It's a little plot of land just outside the kitchen door where the Mistress grew greens and carrots and corn and squash and onions and sweet taters.

"Massa would go hunting for rabbits and deer in the thick forests around the cabin. Sometimes he took the boys fishin'. I can still remember the mouth-waterin' smell of fried catfish. It was served with yellow corn so sweet it was like someone poured sugar all over it. We also licked our chops over mustard and dandelion greens cooked in fatback, along with buttery cornbread to sop it up. We always had plenty of good food to eat, 'cept during the war, when Yankees and Rebs stole everything in sight. I'll tell you lots of interesting stories about the war another evening."

Out of the blue, a little voice asked, "Where were your parents, Grandma?"

That snapped me out of my reverie and forced me to deal with another difficult question. My granddaughter couldn't imagine three kids playing all day long without parents supervising their every move—like her parents watched her every step.

"You see, we didn't know our parents. The boys were sold to the Stalnaker family, perhaps from birth, as was I. Then I was sold again at the age of twelve for the paltry sum of one dollar. I didn't even know who my mother was until I came here to Barnesville and learned of her name from my father."

How does one explain all that to a youngster?

— An excerpt from *The Mystery of Margaret Booker*

By Bob Irelan

Bob Irelan's 2018 novel, *Angel's Truth, One Teenager's Quest for Justice,* marks the first time he has knowingly written fiction. But his commitment to writing stretches back to the late 1950s, when he majored in journalism at the University of Maryland.

Following 10 years of newspaper and magazine reporting and writing, including stints at the *Wall Street Journal* and *Nation's Business* magazine in Washington, DC, he spent 32 years in corporate public relations and as a corporate officer for a Fortune 500 family of companies.

In retirement, he taught a public relations course for two years at University of the Pacific and for five years at University of California, Davis, Extension. Each course focused on writing as the quintessential communications tool.

Bob is at work on another novel. He lives with his cat, Jocko, in Rancho Murieta, California and takes correspondence at golfbob@calweb.com.

A Tale of Two Kitties

I had been without a feline pal for six months, so I was vulnerable. Jocko and I had grown old together. He was 18 when he died, I was 83. Measured in "cat years," I figure we were contemporaries. My wife and I adopted him when he was five because his "owner" was terminally ill and anxious to find a happy home for him.

Jocko became a sort of savior because my beloved wife of nearly 50 years died of a massive heart attack less than a year after he became a part of our family. The next 12 years, my live-in companion was this handsome, curious, affectionate black and white tuxedo boy. He never failed to greet me when he heard the garage door go up, or to climb into my lap wherever I sat, or to rouse me awake, most often at the pre-dawn hour of 4:30 a.m. or 5:00 a.m. He persistently taught me his needs and desires. His affection for Skipjack Tuna dictated that I order it in large, heavy, multiple container boxes.

The entire house became his. For a time, he would choose a particular chair as his favorite. But then, after a couple or three weeks, he would move to another room, another chair, another sofa, another bed. Nighttime boredom sometimes produced the tap, tap, tap sound of him opening kitchen cabinet doors.

Jocko and I had a deal. He liked being outdoors. But I feared he would get hit by a car, or wander off, or become dinner for a mountain lion or some other critter if I allowed him that freedom. So, weather permitting, I carried him outside in my arms several times a day for walks around the yard. Upon reaching his favorite tree, I'd hold him up in such a way that he could sharpen his front claws. Neighbors became used to seeing this odd sight.

I went on vacations without him, but always felt a twinge of guilt. He never seemed to mind. Instead of pouting, he would welcome me after ten days as if I had been gone for only an hour or so. Life with him was simple, uncomplicated, joyful.

However, toward the end, Jocko developed a number of serious medical issues. He wasn't himself and clearly did not feel well. After he died, I pretty much decided to move on without anything else alive in the house. I could feel free to travel more frequently and for longer periods without guilt or the expense of a cat sitter. Lock the door. Go. Nothing to worry about.

I am blessed to have an attentive, loving family, part of which is nearby, and wonderful friends, but now, for the first time ever, I was living alone.

Then, during Thanksgiving weekend, it happened: a Facebook posting on my iPhone. It was from Calaveras County Animal Services in San Andreas, California, 40 or 50 miles from where I live. "Adopt Me!" it pleaded. "Calling all tortie aficionados. Bai is a beautiful tortoiseshell with big golden eyes and super-silky coat. She is ten years young, very healthy, and looks and acts like a much younger kitty."

Maturity was important to me. Who knows how much longer I have? I am at the point in life where I no longer buy green bananas, and I check the obituaries every morning to see if mine is among them.

Somewhat reluctantly, I continued to read: "Bai is in the shelter because her caregiver passed away and relatives were unable to give her a home." That tugged at my heartstrings. She had gone from the stability of having a home and a familiar person caring for her to the uncertainty of a strange, constricted setting. I thought more about her age. Not all that many folks want to adopt older animals; most opt for kittens and puppies. I found myself beginning to worry about Bai's fate.

Reading further, I saw where "Bai needs to be indoors only because she has always been indoors. Her ideal home would be with a person or family who will give her lots of love and attention." Older, indoor kitty—those were pluses as far as I was concerned.

However, my emotions continued to be mixed. Was I really interested in acquiring her or was this only a humane impulse aroused by concern for her future?

I phoned the shelter and felt relief initially when the person who answered told me, "Some people are coming today to look at her. If they don't take her, we'll let you know."

Whew! At least I cared enough to inquire. I felt good about having done that.

A couple of hours passed. The phone rang. "Bai's still available. They decided not to take her," the kind voice said. "We will be closing soon and not reopening until Tuesday. If you are interested, call us and you can come then."

That gave me several days to think and to talk repeatedly with my son, Jon, and daughter-in-law, Melissa. Neither of them pressured me, but they were encouraging because they knew I had experienced a deep sense of loss when Jocko passed. I stewed for a while but finally asked Melissa if she would go with me to see Bai.

Tuesday arrived. I phoned Animal Services. Bai was still a resident, so off to San Andreas we went, with the cat carrier that had been Jocko's in the back of the car.

Driving through the Sierra foothills toward San Andreas that morning, I still had not fully committed. I was leaning toward "yes," but still undecided. It would depend on the chemistry of our meeting.

Bai was as advertised: a beautiful girl with golden eyes and a soft coat that is a collage of black, gray, tan, brown, and almost orange. She was understandably a bit uncertain as to who we were and what we wanted but she allowed Melissa to pet her. Then it was my turn. As I petted her, I could hear her purr. That did it.

I don't remember exactly what I said. Maybe it was a simple "Okay, I'll take her." Whatever, we were asked to proceed to another building to fill out the necessary paperwork. Meantime, her shelter caregiver said, "I'll bring her to you after I've said my goodbyes." It turns out Bai had been at the shelter for more than a month and had endeared herself to the caring folks there.

The drive home was uneventful. No meows; no moving around in the carrier. Who knew how Bai would adapt? I, though, was at peace with my decision.

I knew from experience and from reading that relocated cats, especially older ones, initially prefer a single room. With food and a litter box already set up in the master bathroom, I delivered her to the adjoining master bedroom. After a cursory inspection of those surroundings, she opted for under the bed.

Bai chose to trust me rather quickly, but she was spooked by any sudden noise, and for a couple of weeks showed no interest in venturing down the hall to inspect other rooms. The bedroom (especially under the bed) and the bathroom were sufficient, thank you very much.

I stated earlier that Bai was "as advertised." The ad promoting her said, "She loves to have her belly rubbed and shows her appreciation by licking your hand." That turned out to be an understatement. In the weeks and months since, whenever I approach, she collapses on the floor, rolls over on her back, extends her body to its full length, spreads her legs, and expects repeated belly rubs. In return, I get the promised licks. The intense pleasure she clearly feels as she contorts her body to direct my hand to the perfect spot invariably causes me to laugh out loud.

As I write this, Bai and I have been together for nearly five months. She has become more adventuresome, willing to follow me into any room, but is still most comfortable in the "back of the house." She still chooses to be invisible to strangers. I hope and expect that will change with the passage of time, but for now, anyone other than yours truly who wants to see her is invited to crouch down and peer under my bed. I have a flashlight handy for that purpose.

One thing I am sure of: I made the right decision. Bai is a delight. I do all the talking. I even make up songs that include her name and affirm what a pretty girl she is. She is at least tolerant of my off-key vocalizing (it does not cause her to retreat under the bed). She expects a couple of kitty treats and five or ten minutes of belly rubs before I turn out the light at night, a routine we repeat the next morning.

I believe she would agree that life is good.

Bonnie Blue

By Bonnie Blue

Bonnie Gault-Blue recently retired from working as a licensed marriage and family therapist.

She is now writing pieces for the memoir that has haunted her thoughts for the last few years. It is about her time living in a community in Scotland.

In addition, she writes stories about nature.

She has been published by the *New Times* of Seattle.

A Raccoon Tale

Every afternoon I hurried home from high school, changed into a pair of knee-high leather boots, and prepared for an assault of sharp raccoon teeth on my legs. This was a game we played. Cooney lowered into position, then barreled towards me. Tank-like, he was impervious to obstacles or distractions. I taunted, "Oh you can't get me," as I leapt over him, racing around the living and dining rooms.

It had not always gone so easily. A young raccoon needs to exercise his hunting skills and usually does this with other kits in his litter. For Cooney, we humans were his practice prey. After a few painful bites on flesh, I donned my mother's winter boots and transformed annoyance into fun.

When Cooney's aggressive energies were exhausted, he climbed onto the small bed in our living room and settled in to rest, burying his face under a thick tail. It was then my arms could surround him, and I could purr sweet love in his ear. Gathering up the folds of his fat bottom, I lifted, pressing him close. His pudgy paws encircled my neck and his body relaxed into my chest as we walked around the house.

My younger sister, Bu, loved animals, the wilder the better. Once she brought a pair of injured squirrels into our Chicago home. I had to bear with an occasional chase scene that involved squirrels running up my body then leaping onto the curtains or a piece of furniture. Bu had a baby raccoon before Cooney, a gift from my uncle, who found an abandoned kit in his suburban back yard. She kept it in a cage in her room, only letting it out when we were home, which I preferred. Wild animals scared me. There were other creatures that shared our home. But only one took my heart and burst it open.

It was early summer, and I was slow to rise that morning, preferring instead to stay curled up under a blanket, reading Tolkien. My mother knocked on the door.

"Come in," I called out.

"Bonnie, look what we have." The lilt in my mom's voice betrayed her excitement. She and Bu filled the doorway. Tossing my blanket aside, I rolled off the bed, not noticing the holy terror entering my room. A young raccoon rushed in between their well-shod feet, aiming straight towards mine. Suddenly my naked toes felt far too vulnerable.

I screamed and chaos ensued. His attack response was triggered, teeth and claws at the ready. He chased me as I leapt over my study chair, then wove between my mother and sister, who stood calmly in the center of the room. Finally, I jumped onto the bed. The raccoon stopped short, unable to climb up my bedspread. My mother and sister were in hysterics.

"Get him out!" I yelled. Bu grabbed him up and both retreated, enjoying my panic much too much. I leaned against my closed door and recovered my breath. *I'm cornered. A wild animal is roaming our halls and clearly my family is okay with it.*

Could I ever get used to him? Would I ever feel safe around him? Despite the warm day, I dressed, putting on pants and leather shoes. Then I ventured out to face the beast.

Cooney was never put in a cage. He lived with us like a family pet. I was the last to recognize his pet status, staying well-defended behind thick clothing and at a cautious distance.

My heart softened quickly. I had no choice. I could not ignore his antics, or pretend he wasn't the best entertainment in or outside our house. I learned his rhythm. He slept all night and into the day and woke full of energy about the time I came home from school.

My favorite time was when he was sleepy. My school was close, so during lunch break I often walked home to find Cooney nestled between Bu's mattress and box spring. He had the ability to flatten, making it through surprisingly small spaces. After pulling himself inside, he circled till his nose faced outwards for fresh air while he slept.

I lifted the corner of the mattress, then softly stroked the hairs on his paws and nose. Eventually he stretched, yawned, and rolled over so I could rub his belly.

He loved when I scratched the fur on his ringed tail, especially the juncture near his back. He returned my grooming efforts by running his nails through my hair or lightly biting the surface of my arms to get any fleas that might be there. It was these quiet moments that forged our bond.

My sister slept with him every night. One time I joined them. He crawled to the end of her bed, nipping my feet to get more room. I never did that again. A nighttime of nibbled toes was not worth the cuddling.

Cooney used a box of kitty litter, but, to my mother's consternation, he cleansed himself by dragging his bottom along the carpet afterwards. At times he climbed onto the toilet seat, as if to try out what we did. What captivated him was the bowl of water below. He made it his practice to leap up after a flush and watch the water disappear and fill up again.

When I took a bath, he tried to join me, balancing on the rim, running his paws through the water. "Mom, can you get Cooney out of here?" I was afraid he might jump in. I imagined floating fur coating my scratched and punctured body.

His hunting trips took him deep into the kitchen. After school, Bu and I usually made a bee line to the refrigerator. Cooney caught on. One day he followed close behind and leapt inside. He vise-gripped the bottom shelf and slid into position, flattening to fill the space. Despite our attempts to grab his hind legs and pull, he clung to the metal rack. We had to remove every food item from the shelves to dislodge his interest.

One day, I heard the banging of falling pans. Cooney was exploring the lower cabinets, a long open space with doors for access. The scent of cereals called to him, but they were in a drawer. Our cookware suffered his mining efforts.

Occasionally I found Cooney sitting upright on the overstuffed chair in the living room, trying to get peanut butter fragments out of an empty jar or licking yogurt residue from an old container. I could see in the distance a cornucopia of garbage from the trash can he had tumbled across the kitchen floor.

Cooney was also not above grabbing food directly from us. One dinnertime, I engaged in a tug of wills with him over my pork chop, which he had skillfully slipped from my plate as I prepared to put my knife and fork into it.

Cooney was a natural climber with very little to climb. Our Christmas tree was sacrificed to the little bandit. He had gained a lot of weight by wintertime, which is natural for raccoons who lived in snowy areas. Our tree never stood a chance. We lifted it upright time and time again.

Visitors learned to be vigilant with their possessions around our raccoon. Cooney followed every intriguing scent; penetrated every defense. He ripped through the lining of a friend's pea jacket to get to the cigarettes in his pocket. Another day, another friend saw her purse breached, a shredded joint lying in pieces on the couch. "Hey, I was looking forward to smoking that," she said.

One evening I came home to find Cooney rapidly pawing the wool bedspread. His eyes glowed green as if possessed.

"Mom, what happened to Cooney?"

"That rascal found my diet pills," she answered. "They were hidden in a medicine bag in the hall closet. The whole bag was ripped apart. I have no idea what else he ate." Worried, we watched him carefully. A few hours later, he began to slow down.

Each bit of destruction taught us greater care in storing our things. Like a hyperactive child, he tore through areas of our house we assumed were safe and secure. Anticipating his next exploration was never possible. We were always one step behind. The force of his wild curiosity dominated our house.

Cooney escaped once when the front door was left ajar. We hurried out. We finally spotted him in our back alley, up a large tree. From the heights, he watched us bribe him with gooey sweet rolls and savory bacon. We called out, "Cooney... come on boy," altering our voices to induce him to come down. Nothing worked. It was a cold night with a sleeting rain. I lay in bed, worrying. Is he okay? Would I ever see him again?

The next morning, I opened the front door, and there he sat, shivering and wet. I grabbed him up in a towel and carried him to my sister's bed. He slept through the day and into the next, occasionally sneezing, his nose dripping.

In contrast to my increasing love for him, my mother's relationship with Cooney went off in another direction. It began with the vacuum cleaner. He hated that machine.

"Bu, come and get this raccoon. I'm trying to vacuum." Cooney was biting wherever he could find soft items, which included her legs and feet.

It was annoying cleaning our white World Book encyclopedia covered in grape jam paw prints. The green globs on the carpet leading to a tube of green oil paint was one of my mother's 'last straws.' As winter turned into spring, Cooney's aggression towards her increased. Whenever she returned home, he lowered into attack position and chased her into her bedroom. She was beginning fear him.

"That raccoon has gotta go," she ordered. We didn't want to hear it but had to accept the inevitable. He was becoming an adult, showing more aggression by the day.

One spring afternoon, my father drove to our house with a borrowed cage in his back seat. We planned to drop Cooney off at an animal sanctuary in a forest preserve. My heart was breaking as I gathered him up. He wrapped his arms around my neck, trusting me, as he had done so many times before. I carried him to the car. He pushed off from my arms, not sure what was happening, but we managed to cage him. Bu and I sat on either side. As we drove away, he paced, trilling his unhappiness while testing the edges of the cage for weakness.

"It's okay, Cooney," I said softly, trying to keep my voice steady, "It's okay."

So many things were wrong that day. Cooney had never been in a car. He had never been in a cage. What kind of cage could hold a raccoon? We didn't know. This cage door had a single latch in the middle. Cooney managed to get the door askew enough to start to squeeze through one side of the opening. We pushed his arms back in, but the latch gave way. My sister threw her body over the opening, hoping her weight would keep the door shut, but that raccoon was relentless. At first his paws and arms emerged, then his face, and then the rest of his body slid from under her. I tried to redirect him, but he bit my hand, drawing blood. All of this occurred in silence. It would not help to upset our father, who lived in the suburbs and had never met a raccoon before.

I had to inform him, "Uh, Dad, Cooney is out of the cage. We'll hold him in our laps."

My father was furious. "What!" He was driving out to the suburbs with a loose raccoon in his car.

We took turns restraining Cooney, trying to keep him calm, all the while tears of sadness streamed down our faces. Time and again we pulled him back from exploring the rear window or climbing onto the front seat.

I knew how hard this was for all of us. But it was not a time for reflection; it was a time for forcing one foot in front of the other. Only later did I wonder, would he survive in the wild, not having the guidance of a mother.

It was darkening as we pulled into the parking lot of a nature preserve. A wildlife center next to a pond was off to the right. The forest surrounded us. Bu carried Cooney and I carried supplies down a hiking path till we were deep enough in to release him. Off the path a bit, I laid out a cardboard box with an old towel for bedding, a bowl with water and a bag of cat kibble. We hoped he would transition to other food when he found his bearings.

As soon as my sister laid him down, we took off running. He immediately followed us, emerging into the clearing, only to be stopped short by a woman walking a dog. This was something new for him.

Just as I entered the car, I looked back one last time. He was watching us curiously, one paw raised. I closed the door and we drove away.

Kavanaugh

Larry

By Larry Kavanaugh

Larry Kavanaugh had a long career as a faculty member, administrator, and research leader at California Community Colleges and was a founding dean of a community college center on the Mendocino Coast.

He has published several articles nationally about travel in various parts of the world.

He is also a practicing—"*Practicing* is the right word," he says—poet, but none of his poetry has been published. He spends much time ruminating about why?

They Lie Still

On a high-energy and fun-filled tour of Italy we had a sobering morning. We stopped at the Florence American Cemetery and Memorial to visit the graves of 4,402 young Americans who made the ultimate sacrifice. They gave their lives and spilled their blood on foreign soil to help assure millions of Americans would not have to spill theirs on American soil.

The tidy rows of white crosses flow across a gentle rise and up to a dignified marble building and an immense granite wall where the names of the Americans buried there are listed. Sprinkled among them are graves, specifically marked, of several Medal of Honor recipients. The grass is intensely green and manicured by the Italian groundskeepers, almost as if each blade was at attention, saluting the price each young American paid. A breeze blew up the slope, ruffled the flags, and made leaves on the trees tremble. Dark clouds, the first we had seen in Italy, seemed to fill the sky.

The young men, and a few women, who lie interred here probably never took the time to look at the sky as they fought and slogged their way through the streets of Rome; or through the mud of Santerno Valley; or scaling the rocky cliffs of Futa Pass in 1944 and 1945. They were probably more interested in keeping their heads down and out of harm's way.

As I looked out over the acres of crosses, some decorated with the Star of David, I couldn't help but think it must be a comfort to these fallen to know with certainty who the enemy was and that the enemy was evil. They knew the Axis must be defeated. They knew the American way of life was in jeopardy. Their brave and steadfast pursuit of enemy forces—paid for in blood—did sound the death knell for Hitler and his maniacal dream of world domination. What a loss that they fell so near the finish line. We know the Nazis and their cohorts were defeated. Small comfort to them, indeed.

I felt even connected to those soldiers and airmen when I found listed on the granite wall a soldier with my surname. He was Sgt. Charles E. Kavanaugh of Indiana. Although he was no relation, I felt connected. I couldn't find his grave to pay my respects, but this faceless relative and his comrades were on my mind all that day.

A carefree day of travel was transformed into a day of caring and mourning, as the Italian cemetery guide, the bus driver, our tour guide, and 42 American tourists from many parts of the U.S. spent an hour with many young Americans who gave their lives defending our freedom. Veteran's Day was months off, but for us this was a day for remembering veterans.

Despite the threatening clouds, the day stayed dry. However, hardly an eye was. We felt the palpable cost of freedom in a land thousands of miles away.

By Kiyo Sato

Kiyo Sato, nurse, military veteran, and mother of four, wrote of her family's experience of being swept off to a concentration camp and ultimately surviving and succeeding.

Dandelion through the Crack garnered high praise and numerous awards, including the William Saroyan Prize for International writing (2008) and the NCPA Best Overall Book Award (2008).

The Smithsonian Institution invited Kiyo to speak at their Asian Pacific American Program, which marked the 67th anniversary of the signing of Executive Order 90666 and the subsequent imprisonment of 120,000 Japanese Americans.

While serving in the Air Force, she earned the rank of Captain and completed her nursing education. As a civilian public health nurse, Kiyo developed the Blackbird Vision Screening System to detect eye problems in young children.

Glimpses

D
id someone ever peek into your diary? Well, would you believe, in my case it wasn't a younger brother curious to know what secrets he might discover. Would you believe it was the FBI?

Japan bombed Pearl Harbor and I became a possible spy. Go figure.

First of all, how did I manage to last so long? In a couple of years, I'll be one hundred years old.

Heavens!

Watch your step, I keep reminding myself. At this age you could break a leg which could be the beginning of my end.

Let me ask you this: if you were to choose one piece out of your diary to write about what would that be?

I had no trouble: May 27, 1942, the day I became a non-alien and prisoner #25217-C. That number is tattooed, not on my arm, but in my brain until I die. I must confess, it is not written down. Since the FBI agent read my diary, I was afraid to write anything.

Mind you, I was born in Sacramento, California. I am an American citizen.

I thumb through my box full of journals and composition tablets. Seventy years later I am in Washington DC speaking at the Smithsonian. A message comes from Mr. David Haberstich, Director of the Smithsonian Historical Archives.

"Please stop by."

My daughter and I are escorted into a glassed-in cubicle and instructed to put on white gloves as if we are about to touch the ancient, archaeological objects of the dead.

A tray of letters is carefully placed on the table. To my amazement, they are my letters—letters I had written from Poston Concentration Camp II to Miss Cox, my Edward Kelley School teacher. In the stack, I also find my brother's beautifully written letters, and more from her other pupils. The tiny country school with a belfry, established in 1869, was a safe place in an unsafe world in Sacramento County for her fifty-two children.

"How did these letters get here?" I ask Mr. Haberstich.

The story unfolds:

I had applied to be released from the Poston, Arizona, concentration camp to continue my education. What I thought would be a simple procedure had not been so. A Military Intelligence Officer, Gerald Lamboley, was assigned to investigate my case. He had come all the way to Mills, California, to question Miss Cox, who by then had only thirteen students. He confiscated sixty letters written to her from Poston Camp II.

After the war, when he was no longer employed, he felt he had important documents in his hands. He called the Smithsonian.

"I wish I could have talked with him," I mention to Mr. Haberstitch.

After my return home, I receive a call from Dr. Gerald Lamboley himself. He is ninety-four years old, only a few years older than me. We have a friendly chat.

"You people lived under those horrendous conditions," he tells me. "Someone should write about it."

"Apparently you haven't read my book," I tell him.

I mail him a copy of *Dandelion Through the Crack: A Japanese American Family's Quest for the American Dream*, which received the William Saroyan International Prize for Writing in 2008.

Regretfully, I haven't heard from him since.

I've often wondered what prompted him to apply for his job. Did he expect to prove me a spy? Did he believe, as did so many others, that my father bought land by Mather Air Field in preparation for this war? Was it a disappointment that after four years of internment that not a single case was brought against the prisoners in the concentration camps? Was he relieved?

It may surprise you to know that eight men were indicted as spies, all of them white, and all of them from outside the camps.

If General John L. DeWitt, the designer of our ten American concentration camps had said: "I was wrong" and apologized, what a heavy burden he would have lifted from our country, and what an inspiration it would be for the world that was still reeling from Hitler's carnage.

Have we made progress as a human race?

Racism continues. Never mind who created this hierarchy. When you stop to think, it's a rather dumb idea—judging people by their skin color. I'm sort of brownish and belong somewhere in-between. According to Dr. Michio Kaku, physicist, humans are at their lowest rung of development. He might be right. We kill any person of a certain color we don't like.

We cry for our children, but more importantly we need to cry for our perpetrators. They are the product, be it Hitler, DeWitt, Pol Pot, the mass shooters, the bullies and more, of their lack of proper nurturing in early childhood, and perhaps very likely, abuse.

Kodomo-no-tameni, for the sake of children, we reminded each other. Give children the best of us, even if it is to just hold the hand of a lost and crying child and go from barrack to barrack to find his family.

Someone started baseball at the firebreak for the youngsters. I helped gather little children for a nursery school in an empty barracks room. A piano teacher started a class. My younger sister's first lesson was to draw a keyboard on which to practice.

While the outside world raged with hate, we children quietly survived following our elders.

Contemplating my long life, thumbing through my diaries, I ask myself: What was the best part? Without a doubt it was from birth to fifteen years.

What was the worst part? May 27,1942. I'm still talking to students. Erasing history will not correct racism.

Remember *Kodomo-no-tameni* wherever we are. We must get back on track towards a caring and humane society where children do not have to be told, "Beware of strangers." Start with a smile for the next child you encounter.

Marc Townsend

By Marc Townsend

Born on the East Coast but raised in the West, Marc Townsend has always loved to read and learn about people, places, and things.

He says, "My thirst for knowledge lends itself to the creative outlet of wanting to share what I know with others in the form of writing."

He tends to write in a non-fiction, narrative way, and currently he is completing a memoir about his two lives—one in which he was raised up in a fundamental, conservative religious environment, and the other in dealing with an addictive compulsion, subsequent recovery while forging a new path forward.

The One Thing
They Won't Forget

There are some experiences in life that just stick with you. One of mine came courtesy of Victor, my friend VJ's dad, who had become something of a father figure to me.

One morning when we were out early morning preaching to people on the streets, Victor decided it was a good time to teach me, my friend Danny, and his two boys a life lesson. He waved us over enthusiastically and said, "Hey, I want to show you guys something. But before I do, think about this. What's the most precious thing you have?"

Victor was good at making us think about stuff like that. He was at his emotional best when a tear would well up in his eyes. His raw emotion always left an impact. We knew he cared about us.

For teenagers, the most precious thing could be anything. "My egg McMuffin," VJ said clutching his greasy Mickey D's bag like his life depended on it.

"My relationship with Jehovah," I said. I was always serious about God. Motioning to the car, Victor exhorted, "Come on, let me show you something."

We all loaded back into his Acura sedan. He drove us to what was then known as Alexian Brothers hospital in east San Jose. I don't know how he did it since it was for family only, but he got us up to the hospital nursery where we could see the newborn babies.

"See all these babies? Look at them. So beautiful and innocent. They have their whole lives ahead of them. Hopefully, they have a loving family to care for them well. Right now, they have everything to look forward to in life. See, they've even been given names."

"But hey, you know what? You know what they don't have?" he motioned us to lean in as we listened with bated breath.

"They have no reputation." Victor always had a game plan to his lessons. Once again, he caught us in his web of intrigue. We were eager to see how this one ended.

"Come on, let me show you something else."

Two miles down the road we found ourselves pulling into the Calvary Catholic Cemetery. We kids weren't freaked out by cemeteries. We'd been taught the dead don't exist anymore except in God's memory, so we weren't afraid of ghosts or anything. Demons maybe. But not ghosts.

After we all got out of the car, Victor pointed to a gravestone. "Hey, look at this tombstone. So, and so. 1922 to 1956. He died young. Look at this one: So, and so, 1930 to 1975. Some of these died young, some lived a long life."

It was a bit sobering to see end dates on lives. Even for us invincible youngsters who thought we'd live forever.

"All these people buried here came into the world just like those babies back in the nursery. And they all were given names" he said. "See that dash between the birth date and day of death? What do you think that represents?" We all pondered that for a moment. "That dash represents their lives and the reputations they died with. What do you think this guy's reputation was when he died? Or, what about this woman here? What kind of name did she make for herself?"

Victor paused to let the questions sink in. There were hundreds of graves. We were imagining the different lives all these souls might have had lived. We figured most were probably good people. Maybe some had done bad things though.

Another question broke the silence. "When you hear the name Hitler, what do you think of?"

"How he killed people," Danny said. "We think of his bad reputation."

"That's right. He was given a name at birth but by the end of his life he'd made a bad name for himself." But think about the good name Jesus made for himself, or other faithful ones of old.""

"So, when it comes down to it all we have to show for our lives is a dash on a gravestone?" I asked.

Victor put his hand on my shoulder and said, "Paco, more important than that is the reputation we have before God."

He always called me Paco. Then he turned to us with a serious look on his face. And as he cleared the lump in his throat asked, "Hey, what kind of name do you guys want to make with God?"

I have always cherished the lesson I learned that day from Victor. Though I haven't always been a sterling example of how to live righteously. He helped me appreciate that in life, we're all works in progress. As such, I often reflect on the type of name I'm making with God. I owe that to Victor.

I'm no longer a Jehovah's Witness. But I will always be a child of God. As such, I do my best each day to make a good name for myself and build a good reputation.

Maya Angelou once said she learned that people will forget what you said, people will forget what you did, but people will never forget how you made them feel."

Think about the effect we have on the people around us each day. Whatever I do, I try to leave a feeling of goodwill with whomever I connect. I urge you to do the same. Try. Things don't always go as planned. People don't always act right. We can't control the things around us, but we can control ourselves. We can convince ourselves to always do the right thing in any given circumstance.

By Larry Mandelberg

Larry Mandelberg is a consultant, speaker, and author. A natural problem solver, Larry represents the fifth generation of his family's business.

He is an effective catalyst for change and has published more than 80 newspaper columns. His first book was *Businesses Don't Fail, They Commit Suicide*.

A sought-after speaker, he has delivered more than 60 business-changing keynotes and workshops. He has been a guest on television and radio programs talking about business and entrepreneurship.

Through his consulting practice, he provides leadership development, executive coaching, ethics training and strategic planning to mid-sized B2B organizations in multiple industries.

Larry has launched four start-ups, led a merger, and performed a successful turnaround.

He has been a regular contributor to the *Sacramento Business Journal.*

The Case of the Plagued Patriarch

"Your beliefs become your thoughts. Your thoughts become your words. Your words become your actions. Your actions become your habits. Your habits become your values. Your values become your destiny." —Mahatma Gandhi

• • •

In the seventeen months since joining the firm, Brit Poole was no stranger to the room—an environment she was certain had been designed to intimidate. The regal cherrywood table, leather-bound books, high-backed chairs, and scent of power-generated pheromones seemed to warn every interloper, here lives a presence to be reckoned with.

Poole entered the room to find founding partner, Willard Kronick and his five power partners, seated in their decreed places along with a dozen or so attorneys looking primed and ready for court. Yet something was different. She felt it the moment she came in for this morning's ad hoc meeting. An unfamiliar presence of uncertainty was in this familiar place with familiar faces—the conference room of Sanborne, Hollande & Kronick.

After 40 years of hard work, all the pieces were finally falling into place and the firm was growing like a weed. Their decades of success and legal experience made SHK one of the most respected in town. In the last two years, staff expanded from 65 to over 250. It sounded great and felt terrible.

The rapid growth had given rise to a certain loss of control, and for attorneys, that's never a good thing. An uncomfortable, unfamiliar feeling lurked throughout the dark corners of their offices. They couldn't tell if a grain of sand had found its way into their oyster to make a pearl, or if the firm was about to implode. Either way, it felt prickly, and Brit could tell she was about to be forced to face it head on.

"I'm troubled," the patriarch opened the meeting. "I'm distressed by our rapid growth. It feels like we're growing too fast, and I'm worried about our reputation. I know growth is critical, but it feels like all these new people are putting us at risk. How are we going to make sure we don't endanger our reputation?"

Randy Schneider, one of the firm's most successful partners, was visibly bothered by Kronick's comments.

"Willard," Randy said, "our clients are thrilled and we're having our best year ever, yet I'm feeling a lot of anxiety. What is going on?"

"Randy..." Kronick said, "It's times like this when everything seems to be humming along that I worry the most. I feel I'm missing something. A law firm doesn't succeed just because it's providing good counsel. How we do business, our values, our ethics, how we treat our clients, these things can get away from us. When our growth exceeds our ability to manage it, we're in trouble."

The Managing Partner, Martin Grange, responded, "Walter, I see no evidence of a problem. Has HR given you any reason to be concerned? It's not like you to raise an issue like this out of the blue. I'm not seeing or hearing anything from staff or clients that worries me. What do you see the rest of us aren't seeing?"

"What kind of support and oversight is happening with our new people?" Kronick answered. "Can anybody in this room tell me they know whether our new staff is even capable of representing us the way we want to be represented?"

Bob Gaiety was generally considered their most successful and respected rainmaker. If anybody should be concerned, Bob would be that guy.

"Willard," Gaiety began, "I do not have your level of concern. It doesn't sound like you're worried about a problem with our new people, it sounds like you want proof we can handle our growth without losing who we are and what we stand for."

"That's exactly what I'm concerned about."

As the only one in this meeting who was part of the growth Willard was referring to, Brit felt everyone was waiting for her to say something. She wasn't quite sure how honest she could be.

"I'll admit, I was a bit lost when I started last year," she said to Kronick. "I was given all the history—how you, Sanborne and Mr. Hollande began, and I was proud to be joining the firm. But once I came on board, I never felt like part of a team. Our values have always bothered me," she said.

"What?" Several people murmured while looking at each other with raised eyebrows.

"We have them posted all over the office," Brit explained, "but what exactly does teamwork mean? Does it mean my team does my busy work for me? What does reliability, trustworthiness and transparency mean to you and how are they supposed to affect the way I do my work, the way I interact with clients or our staff? How do I know if I'm doing it your way? How do any of us know if we have an accurate understanding of what you want from us?"

"Fair point," said Gaiety. "Not sure how we might be able to do that. If we could do it in a way that didn't make people feel like they were being watched, like big brother was waiting to pounce on them for the tiniest slip up, if it could be done in a positive manner, I don't see how it would hurt."

Mary Sanchez, one of the more respected partners Brit didn't know very well, spoke up.

"I have a tech client that does something I've been intrigued by ever since I found out about it. They only have 25 or 30 people so they're not as big as we are, and they have a company meeting every Monday for lunch. They serve pizza for everyone, employees and contractors, full and part time. When their vendors are in town they're also welcome to join.

"They open the meeting by going down their list of values. They read each one and talk about it. I was there the other day when they brought up one about honesty. I think it reads, 'We value Honesty.' After they read each value statement, people start telling stories about how they demonstrated that value during the week."

Mary took a moment to gather her thoughts. "I was there recently when a project manager for a multi-million-dollar project they were working on for a Fortune 50 firm, one of their bigger clients, told an honesty value story he had been involved in. His project got behind schedule and his entire development team was starting to stress out. The project manager went to the client and told them the moment he knew they were going to miss a deadline. This was way before any due dates had been missed before there was any sign of trouble or delay. They just knew they weren't going to make the deadline and wanted the client to know as soon as possible.

Now the whole room was focused on Mary.

"Many of you know that's not the way IT firms operate," she said.

"The common reaction is to wait until the deadline is missed, then tell the client there's going to be a delay. Not these guys. They were proud to be late, and I think it was because they had good reason. He told the story about their explanation for the delay and how the client reacted. The client was thrilled and couldn't believe the integrity shown in being up front with them, making sure the delay didn't come as a surprise. It gave everyone time to analyze, review and adjust. They revisited all the project milestones, renegotiated the elements that needed to be adjusted and quickly got back on track, well before anything went south. It's not hard to imagine why that client has become a great referral source and a fierce supporter.

"Turns out, the way they manage their culture is by focusing on their values and making them come alive by sharing stories every week. By asking staff for examples of how those values are brought to life in their daily activities. The meaning of their values really comes to life when they're described through stories of daily activity.

"Maybe we should start doing something like that?" she offered.

Cheryl Romo

By Cheryl Romo

Cheryl Romo is an award-winning investigative journalist and essayist.

She's the former editor of *Common Cause Magazine* in Washington, D.C.; the editor of The *Fortnightly Magazine* in Arlington, VA; and served as the editor of *Sacramento Magazine*.

As a novelist, she's involved in several projects and her first novel, *Ruby Hands,* involves the apparent murder of a young mother on an Arizona Indian reservation. Published by Sowilo Press, *Ruby Hands* was the recipient of the prestigious Eludia Award.

Romo is also co-author of *Biting the Bullet,* an anthology published by Chatterhouse Press.

Dead Reckoning

There was no blood or gore here. Yet the Louvre and its antiquities created a foggy mood that encompassed the senses setting the stage for flight. One room smelled like death on a hot summer's day. Looking at the mummies in the Egyptian collection, I felt the presence of the undead and broke out in a sweat.

Signaling to my companion that I felt unwell, we left the museum and stepped outside for fresh air. It took a few minutes of deep breathing while sitting on a park bench before I began to realize what had happened. I concluded it was a flashback, a moment in time displaced. Seeing ancient caskets inside thick glass cases reminded me of a recent experience I'd hoped had been left behind.

Before coming to Paris, the City of Light, I'd been treading in the underbelly of Los Angeles, the so-called City of Angels. I'd been existing, if you can call it that, in a personal black dungeon where no one speaks, except with rancid and sweet smells. As a professional researcher, I'd done several local history studies and had always been able to complete my work with a sense of detachment. But working with the dead was different. In my artless fashion, I thought I'd escaped their embrace, only to be reminded in an instant of clarity, that the captured never escape. I did smell death on the second floor of a Paris museum once the palace of French kings, and believed the odor had chased me halfway across the world.

Paris was supposed to be a romantic holiday, a two-week sojourn in France with my lover. I was exhausted after spending months researching a county crematory and a paupers' cemetery in Los Angeles—the remains of the lost, poor, and unwanted that had been burned and buried in mass graves more than a century ago. In the beginning, I thought the job was simply to research and document the activities of caretakers who tended the bodies. I didn't anticipate having to fight a reluctant county bureaucracy. Yet, in hindsight, the battle for access was the easy part.

Once inside the human disposal system, I found the caretakers to be gentle, quiet men working in a hell indescribable to anyone who has never experienced their grim world. They were kind gentlemen and I learned from them how to show dignity and respect for the dead.

They warned me to protect myself from unseen danger and I took to wearing a sentimental silver cross around my neck each day. As it turned out, the caretakers were right. The dead lingered and communicated. In their quiet way, they spoke to me of unfulfilled lives, lost hope, and timeless anger. At night, they visited me in my dreams, often wearing face masks, funny hats and carrying parasols to hide their identities. They often made me laugh. I learned to face them down with humor. I took to calling them my "bardo" souls, the lost and afraid who wander without end.

When sometimes mangled bodies, wrapped in simple white sheets, were brought in from the nearby county morgue to the backdoor of the big barn building where ovens burned, I watched as the caretakers handle the lifeless souls with great tenderness.

Most of the time, I worked alone in the adjacent Art Deco chapel, a small church that appeared not to have been used for funeral services in decades. Sitting in wooden pews or standing at the non-denominational pulpit, I ignored the floating human ash— thick as paste—while I methodically read through the "books of the dead," and extracted vital information for my research. The handwritten logs, which began in the late nineteenth century, recorded names, birth to death dates, and the causes of demise for thousands of Angelinos, many of them immigrants, orphaned children or the very poor who died alone. So, as the furnaces belched and the sound of bodies crackled in the next room, I copied information from the death books onto steno pads. No matter how thick the air became, I thought the chapel and everything about it beautiful.

It was my sanctuary.

I drove home at the end of each day with ink-stained fingers, covered in dust and soot. I took hot showers and tried to scrub death away. It was impossible. It was futile; I was branded. In time, I acquired a raspy cough that wouldn't go away, and soon became a vegetarian after finding meat disgusting.

Still, that was the least of it. Part of my work included research at the medical examiner's office and the county morgue. One disturbing memory involved the indignity of seeing a lovely white-haired grandma, nude on a gurney, waiting in a crowded hallway with a line of corpses demurely covered with white sheets. Grandma was next in line for the autopsy table. The medical examiner wore a Donald Duck beanie hat with a twirling propeller on top.

Another disturbing memory was passing by a windowed room. It was like looking into a glass box. A badly burned mother and her two children rested on touching gurneys. I was told by an official the mother and children were victims in a fire deliberately set. One doesn't erase such images.

While my examination of life's aftermath was designed as a short-term project, it became something of an obsession. I felt I was on a mission and that studying indigent death was another way of looking at history, especially in a huge metropolis, like Los Angeles—a city that prides itself on progress and opportunity. In the shabby facilities, I now understood, county leaders didn't want outsiders to see the underbelly of a place where illusions reign supreme and darkness is deliberately perpetuated.

Fading ink is all that remains of the legacy of hundreds of thousands of unfortunate people whose cremations were dutifully recorded, like handwritten real estate transactions, now in crumbling logbooks. But the record books of those buried in L.A.'s paupers' field turned out to be incomplete.

Many names had been lost or never recorded. Expediency reigned and many of the dead—who may have been homeless, child runaways, murder victims or suicides—were never identified. No one sent them kisses or flowers or mourned at their graves. In some cases, no one even knew of their passing.

After I completed the job, I had come to do, I felt adrift. In time, the point of my research became clear. The pauper's cemetery was largely torn apart to make way for a shiny-new subway line. After the digging began, embarrassed county officials puzzled over what to do with all the pesky bones that kept popping out of the ground. The bones weren't supposed to be there. Old maps revealed nothing. Who were these interlopers? No one knew and no one really seemed to care.

Most of the people who came before us have been forgotten, especially if they were considered unremarkable by whatever measure society places on such things. We honor family members. We remember the famous and the infamous. How we treat the memory of all ancestors—even those whose dreams were unrealized—says something about how we, as a society, treat our living?

Plato, the Greek philosopher, believed we are anchored by chains of recollection. In my view, it is his "memory of justice" that is a lesson for how we humans ought to treat one another—dead or alive.

So, like any responsible adult running away from too much reality, I jumped on a plane and escaped with my mate, expecting wine and roses, romance, and culture. By chance or fate, I stumbled upon the once-wealthy Egyptians at the Louvre and bolted into the streets of Paris. My quest for meaning began.

My next tourist stop found me face-to-face with the indignant dead of France. Les Catacombes is a man-made, underground cavern opened to the public in 1810. It was created so the old cemeteries of Paris could be emptied to make room for the living. This subterranean graveyard—commonly called "the empire of the dead," is the final resting place for six million (six million!) humans whose bones were dug up and put on display as part of a gaudy attraction that feels like a theater of the macabre. Most of the bones belonged to Parisians who died in poverty or while fighting wars the living no longer cared to remember—Napoleon's army among them. In Les Catacombes, human bones are stacked and glued together in creepy sculptures. There are "theme" rooms. In other words, here we have the skull and crossbones' room and over here the thigh room and over there the femur room and over here and on and on.

The air was humid and stifling underground and by the time we left, I could barely breathe from the smell of death. That night I had a disturbing dream. I was wandering through the tunnels of Les Catacombes and the dead—who told me they were once soldiers—were speaking to me through a series of lucid images. They indicated they were unhappy and wanted their bones removed from public view. Strangest of all, they wanted their remains covered by plaques in the shape of white rectangles. They didn't mind, they said, being together. A degree of simple dignity was their only request and nothing else would suffice. I must admit I liked them and promised to try and do something to help them.

When I told my skeptical lover about the odd dream, he suggested we go to Hawaii on our next vacation. "You're creating things that don't exist," he said.

Okay, so I'm a little weird, but I couldn't help thinking of Los Angeles and its new subway and all those bones being unearthed just so the living can move a little faster. After several days of wining and dining and bickering, we left Paris to explore the fertile countryside where every

French village seemed to honor and respect its ancestors; particularly those killed during wars. Local cemeteries were unfailingly well-tended and there was an obvious reverence for the departed in this Catholic country.

One of the most impressive sites was the Memorial de Verdun, an enormous mausoleum for French soldiers killed during World War I. On the day of our visit, the facility was crowded with elementary school children waving flags and carrying bouquets of flowers. They were holding a memorial service for the war dead, and the children sang songs and placed their flowers near the flag stands. Pressed to the back of the onlookers, I stood against a marble wall to watch the ceremony. I happened to turn around. Only then did I realize that the walls inside the mausoleum were covered with white rectangle plaques. I pointed out the plaques to my lover and reminded him of his skepticism of my dream, he turned pale. It appeared that Napoleon's forgotten soldiers, whose bones were gawked at in Les Catacombes, had indeed communicated a simple and understated request for eternal privacy and a white memorial plaque.

At that moment, I recalled something I'd forgotten when I stood alone at the paupers' mass graves in Los Angeles. Hundreds were buried together during an annual funeral service organized by the caretakers. Their mass grave was covered by a white rectangular plaque marked with the year of their burial. Even that small token of respect seemed enough to give the lost souls a sense of peace.

By RoseMary Covington

RoseMary Covington Morgan retired from a successful career as a transit planning and development executive manager to accept a new challenge as an author. A lifelong writer, she picked up the pen again nearly four years ago.

More recently, RoseMary published the short story *The Song* in the anthology *Storytellers-Tales* from the Rio Vista Writers' group. She also has three short stories, *My Big Red Shadow, T'was,* and *School Shopping,* plus two poems, published in an anthology compiled by Northern California Publishers and Authors.

She is currently querying about other completed short stores, a novel, and a novella.

RoseMary grew up in St. Louis, Missouri, and has lived in Cleveland, Ohio, and Washington, D.C. She now resides in Sacramento.

Minnow Mildred

Midwestern City, 1958

Her name was Mildred, but because she was born the tiniest of our ever-growing family, we called her Minnow. To the family, she would always be Minnow.

Minnow was a cute, dainty little toddler who sometimes wet her pants, loved to get her hair combed, and reveled in her ability to run. She never crawled and rarely walked; everything was a run—a waddling run, full of joy and giggles.

I was her big sister, ten years old to her almost three. Minnow had been pushed from her place as the baby with the birth of a new little sister so, to help Mother, she was my charge. I loved her like flowers love sunshine. I was her hair comber, her diaper changer, and the person who chased her when she ran. She was my baby doll and the joy of our household.

Most summer evenings, the heat in our house was unbearable, so Mother would take us for a walk until it cooled off. Sometimes, Daddy would join us. Those were special evenings because Daddy would get us ice cream. This evening was more than special. Mother and Daddy piled all of us on a bus for a short ride downtown to look at the store windows—my favorite treat.

Daddy liked to sing, and this evening we belted songs all the way downtown. Minnow clapped her hands, kicked her feet, and tried to sing along. Other people on the bus joined in our fun.

The family rule on our walks was that we stay together. If anyone fell behind, Daddy would give the family whistle and wait until we ran to catch up. My middle sister, aged five, held hands with my brother, aged four. I clasped hands with Minnow. Mother and Daddy also held hands while pushing the baby in her stroller.

We all had our favorite store windows. Mine was any window with mannequins wearing the latest fashions. I hypnotically inspected every garment, pair of shoes, hat, and purse. I would become transfixed, imagining myself wearing the clothes and living in the setting depicted by the window.

Lost in my dream world, I didn't notice Minnow had slipped from my hand and disappeared.

I looked ahead. Mother and Daddy were in front of the home furnishings window. My sister and brother were with them. Minnow was not.

Sweat dripped on my face. I felt my heartbeat pounding in my head. My brain struggled with what to do. I retraced my steps past the toy display window, kitchen wares, and sporting goods. I was running, looking across the street and in front of me until I reached the corner. Although it was a Sunday night, cars were moving swiftly through the streets. Maybe she had been hit. She was so tiny; no one would have noticed. The sweat was running down my face so profusely that I couldn't tell the sweat from the tears.

Daddy's whistle came at the same time I saw a policeman walking toward me. I couldn't let anyone know I'd lost Minnow. *I'm the oldest. She's my responsibility.* Torn between running to Daddy or the policeman, I ran toward the policeman.

Daddy whistled again.

The policeman saw me and quickened his step. The concern in his face said he thought I was injured. When I shouted, "I can't find my little sister, I can't find Minnow," he looked confused.

My body was shaking as I became more desperate with every second. When the policeman calmly said, "You lost your little sister?" I yelled back, "I was holding her hand, and I don't know what happened, but she's gone. I can't find her."

"How old is she?" the policeman asked. I told him her age as he held up his walkie-talkie to call for help.

"She was wearing a blue sunsuit with red straps and blue ruffles on her bottom. She has on white sandals," I said before he could ask.

Daddy was by my side. He must have run to the corner because his shirt was dripping wet. "Daddy, I didn't mean for it to happen. I don't remember when I let go of her hand but, Minnow ran away!"

As the red lights of a police car rounded the corner, I started wheezing. I couldn't catch my breath. The steady voice of the policeman spoke to me, "Calm down, honey. We've got every police officer in the city looking for her. We'll find her."

Mother came with the rest of my family, minus Minnow. She rubbed my back and gave me the apple juice she always kept with her until I stopped wheezing. Daddy had already gone to look for Minnow, and now Mother left to look. "Don't move," she said firmly, looking at my sister, brother, and me. "Don't leave this corner."

By this time, another police car had arrived, and a little crowd had gathered. Soon, downtown looked full of men in blue uniforms and other people calling, "Minnow!"

My younger sister and brother started to cry. "Where's Minnow?" "I want Minnow." Of course, the baby was oblivious to the emergency, but even she was crying.

I was bending over to comfort the baby when I felt someone pull my braid. I turned around to see Minnow, her tiny teeth in a wide smile. As I turned to grab her, she trotted off on her little chubby legs, giggling. She wanted me to chase her. She was playing our game. She would run, and I would try to catch her.

I couldn't leave the other children to chase her this time. But not to worry. She ran right into the open arms of Mother.

Daddy was right behind her with the policeman. After he finished thanking all the people who helped, he gathered me in his arms and gave me a big hug, "You ok?" he asked.

I was grateful I could nod and put my head in the crook of his shoulder. It took a few minutes for everyone to calm themselves and leave downtown. We decided to skip the ice cream and just go home. I held Minnow's hand so tight she constantly complained as we walked to the bus stop.

We found Minnow and rejoiced in our good luck.

As our little family journeyed home that night, we loved Minnow more than ever. We all hugged her. Daddy carried her on his shoulders as we walked from the bus stop to our home.

Forty years later

"Can I warm your coffee?" the smiling server asked for the fourth time. And, for the fourth, time I said yes. My sister was always late, but this was a record—over an hour. I picked up the plastic covered menu lying in front of me, but I couldn't stop watching the window. My eyes shifted to the menu for just a few seconds. In those seconds, she appeared as if by a magic wand.

Minnow had grown into a stunning woman. The kind of beauty that turned heads and stopped conversation. She stopped in front of the door to allow the awe to happen. But it wasn't her beauty that inspired awe today. The beauty had gone. No, it was the recognition that this emaciated woman was out of place even in this simple coffee shop.

Looking for me, she moved, practically twirling, to model the shapeless t-shirt under her smudged blue hoodie. The holes in her jeans didn't appear to be a fashion statement. She removed her knit green/orange striped cap to adjust her lifeless hair before she walked toward my table with shoes that crunched with each step. *Did she know how she looked, or was she high?*

Minnow's first words upon sliding onto the seat across from me, "I can see it in your face, dear sister. No, I'm not high. And don't tell me, 'It's nice to see you' because I know it's not."

I needed to say something. "Where are you living?" *Awkward. Stupid.*

"I don't live, dear sister. I exist. Right now, I am storing my meager belongings in an abandoned building on Fourth Street. You would call it a drug house. My apartment should be available next week, and I'll be out of there."

"Are you working?"

Her stern look was a response to my insensitive statement. "I'm hungry," she said, motioning for the server.

The woman who had been so attentive when serving me coffee was now standing several steps back from the table, haughty, scowling. I was about to say something to her when I remembered: Minnow could do haughty better than anyone outside Hollywood. And she still loved to play.

She began ordering from the sparse coffee house menu in French. When the server looked confused, she switched to German. Then, with a perfect Spanish accent, she ordered three different sandwiches and two salads only to beckon the woman after she placed the order to say she didn't want anything. She clearly enjoyed the farce.

"Let's get out of here, big sis. There's a food truck a block away."

All awkwardness between us faded as we walked to the food truck holding hands. We talked about the family—now all navigating their own families and careers, estranged from

Minnow, "the drug addict." Mother and Daddy had passed on several years before, also estranged from Minnow. but that didn't stop us from trading pleasant stories about our childhood.

We were enjoying our conversation, reaching the food truck faster than either of us wanted. We didn't have to debate our order. "A double serving of French fries," Minnow said.

"Make sure they're hot and squeeze lots of catsup on them," I added.

We walked to a bench in the adjacent park and put the bucket of fries between us. "The best fries in the world are in France and Switzerland," Minnow said, reminding me of her education at the Sorbonne. She continued, giggling, "Except for those fries we used to get from the deli when you walked me home from school."

"Yeah, what happened to lard?" I asked. "These fries are ok, but the plant-based oil they use nowadays takes away some of the decadence and a lot of the taste." We both laughed as we grabbed for the last French fry. She won.

We sat quietly. I was waiting for Minnow to tell me why she called. I expected it to be for money. At least this time, she might ask. The last time I saw her, she stole my wallet from my purse with such skill that it took me days to realize she was the thief. As I began to ask her what she needed, she ran from the bench to a nearby tree to heave the French fries.

I got a bottle of water from my tote bag so she could rinse her mouth. "You're prepared for everything, big sis. Even for an addict trying to begin withdrawal on a stomach filled with greasy French fries."

She seemed to recover but without notice grabbed her stomach, violently shaking. I was trying to hold her close to stop the shaking when a man walked past. "That don't look good, lady. Best call an ambulance."

I did. The ambulance arrived in minutes. The paramedics worked to stabilize her while putting her on a gurney and wheeling her inside the vehicle. I climbed in behind her. While the paramedics inserted an IV and reported her condition to the hospital, I held her hand. I could hear them say drug withdrawal.

They were anxiously yelling questions: "When was the last time you used?"; "What did you take?"; "When did you last eat?"; "Have you peed recently?" I couldn't tell if their reaction was everyday stress but, to me, they seemed unusually tense and worried.

As we arrived at the hospital, Minnow, through labored breaths, pleaded, "I love you, Sis, help me through this. I need you. Please. I need you."

As she pleaded, I saw the face of the little girl I had loved "like flowers love sunshine." As she lay on the ambulance gurney, suffering, crying, fighting for life, I loved my little sister more than ever. I caressed Minnow's hand and held it tightly. This time I wouldn't let her slip away.

LaRonda Bowen

By LaRonda Bowen

CWC's former Sacramento branch president, La Ronda Bowen (bowen.writer@gmail.com), has pursued writing and public policy her entire adult life.

Her areas of expertise include economic development and global warming. She served the U.S. Environmental Protection Agency as an adviser and currently splits her time between Southern California and Sacramento where she is the California Air Resources Board's ombudsman and small business liaison.

Connecting citizens to their government in meaningful ways is her passion. La Ronda has written numerous articles, including topics on environment, business, and health.

With a master of fine arts in creative nonfiction, she belongs to a critique group in Los Angeles County while maintaining her Sacramento branch membership. When not working or writing, La Ronda travels internationally, reminding her that the best recipe for healthy communities is an informed, activist population, a strong small business community, and an open government.

Kryptonite

With a bath-towel draped around her shoulders Superman style, and glossy salt-and-pepper hair hanging down her back, my five-foot, nine-inch, 150-pound grandmother posed for the camera before jumping onto the trampoline at the foot of her rocking chair.

"Suuper Graaan," she shouted as her foster-daughter, Blanca, snapped a picture before dissolving in laughter.

Blanca, now a detective for the Los Angeles Police Department, remembered that morning with delight. "It was the best. Grandaisy was so much fun. When we finished playing, she made us pancakes for breakfast." She was over 80 years old.

This foster mother of twenty, grandmother of nine, and mother of three, was a super-human being, even without her cape.

Grandaisy was born 31 years before Joe Schuster drew the first Superman character and 75 years before Christopher Reeve would play him in *Superman, the Movie*. Despite the age gap, Daisy Todd had a lot in common with Christopher Reeve. Both were champions of the helpless and saviors of children. Both were known by an alias, and both were killed by a silent and underestimated villain—pressure sores.

Reeve was an actor, father, husband, athlete, and activist. He was also an avid horseman. In May 1995, while competing in an equestrian riding and jumping event in Culpeper, VA, Reeve's horse stopped suddenly and propelled Reeves forward. As he fell over his horse, his hands tangled in the bridle, the bit, and the reins. He landed headfirst and although his helmet probably prevented him from suffering brain damage, the impact shattered two of his vertebrae. Reeve was paralyzed from the shoulders down. This Superman was suddenly dependent on others for everything.

In 1995, the year of Reeve's accident, my mother called to tell me Grandaisy had fallen and to meet her at the hospital. She was lying on a gurney, half tilted at an odd angle, her angel face smiling sheepishly.

"I've gone and done it now," she said.

"Yes, I guess you have." I kissed her forehead, sat down beside her, and took her soft, strong hand in mine.

"I know it's bad when old people fall and break their bones," she confided softly.

"We are going to admit her," the doctor said. "She will need hip surgery. The surgeon will come and talk to Grandaisy."

The surgeon arrived. We asked many questions: What were the alternatives? What were the risks? Was Grandaisy too old at 91? Was she too weak after having had a stroke? Would she be able to walk again after surgery?

Hip fractures occur in more than 300,000 Americans annually, 80% of them women. In 2020, the one-year mortality rate after surgery for a broken hip was 21%, but 70% of those who broke a hip, did not have a surgical repair.

Hip fractures increase the risk of dying five to eight times. Pre-existing conditions raise that risk. Common complications are post-operative infections and blood clots. Staying in bed, diabetes, and heart or vascular disease increase an already huge risk of bed sores.

The surgeon assured us that such surgeries were routine and successful, and that even elderly patients quickly regained their ability to walk. He acknowledged that hip repair was major surgery but minimized our concerns about recovery and the fact that Grandaisy was weakened by her stroke a year earlier. He told her to expect to be up and walking within two or three days. He said he had a lot of experience fixing broken hips and referenced a patient even older than Grandaisy who was "doing fine." He assured us that if Grandaisy ever wanted to walk again, surgery was the best thing. We believed him.

We were dependent on full disclosure from the surgeon. But he did not mention the possibility that surgery would result in a lower quality of life, or that the possibility of pressure sores—a common, life-threatening post-operative complication—was probable.

Two-thirds of those who fracture a hip do not return to their pre-fracture level of functioning. Since Grandaisy had not regained her strength after the stroke and was using a four-pronged walker for stability, her chances of being confined to a wheelchair and developing life-threatening pressure sores was high. The surgeon or the hospital team should have given us more information about the reality of problems which could be encountered after a broken hip.

Grandaisy was extremely weak and required blood transfusions following her surgery. It delayed the start of rehabilitation and lessened the likelihood of recovery. Once physical therapy began, Grandaisy's valiant efforts to stand and walk failed.

Just as Grandaisy was hoping to walk again, so was Christopher Reeve. Unlike Grandaisy, Reeve had youth and financial resources on his side; he struggled with paralysis and the numerous complications of spinal cord injury. Reeve threw himself into rehabilitation with superhero determination in preparation for the day a cure would be found. Much to the astonishment of the medical community, Reeve regained some sensation and motion in his body. This brought hope to spinal cord injury and wheelchair-bound patients worldwide. Perhaps those successes kept Reeve's attention diverted from the danger of pressure sores.

A few days before it was time for Grandaisy to be released from the hospital, I removed her white cotton socks and noticed a deep-red sore. I asked the nurse to look at it. A strained expression crossed her face, then made a chart note.

"What is it?" I asked.

"I'll have the doctor look," she replied.

The red spot on Grandaisy's heel was a pressure sore. No one told her, my mother or me what it was, how it formed, how we could prevent it from worsening, or how to stop others sores from developing.

Studies found that about 50% of patients with pressure sores (also known as bed sores, pressure ulcers, or decubitus ulcers) are over the age of 70. Among these, bedsores mean a fourfold increase in the rate of death for the elderly. Many people transferred from hospitals to nursing homes have sores when admitted. Pressure sores are also common in spinal cord injury patients like Christopher Reeve. When pressure sores become infected, they can allow bacteria to enter the blood stream, a condition called septicemia, or they can poison the entire body, a condition called sepsis.

However, pressure sores can be diagnosed by visual observation and if treated early, can be reversed. Preventing pressure sores requires constant vigilance, but once they appear, an integrated approach involving nutrition, physical therapy, medicine, and nursing is needed to cure them.

Pressure sores form where the weight of a person's body presses the skin against a bed, wheelchair, or other firm surface. This pressure temporarily cuts off the blood supply and injures skin cells which die. This injury can occur in a matter of hours.

Unless the pressure is relieved and the blood is allowed to flow to the skin again, the skin soon shows its injury with a patch of redness. If this patch is not protected from additional pressure, blisters form and become open sores. In severe cases, the skin damage creates a deep crater that exposes muscle or bone.

Even though the pressure sore on Grandaisy's heel was a serious problem, the surgeon sent her home. At her follow-up appointment, her regular doctor examined the pressure sore, which the home health nurse had been treating, and insisted my mother take her to a convalescent home of his choosing. He stressed that the facility he recommended employed the best nurses he knew for getting pressure sores to heal.

The convalescent home which the doctor recommended was a nightmare. Patients were allowed to lay in their own urine and feces for hours. Food trays were delivered to patients who could not feed themselves and then taken away untouched.

We were horrified to leave Grandaisy there, and her doctor's assurance that it was the best place for her was of small consolation. Grandaisy never complained. The only question she regularly asked was the heartbreaking one, "When can I go home?"

"As soon as the pressure sore gets well," I would answer, not at all sure when that would be.

The nurse who was the pressure-sore specialist did get the sore on Grandaisy's heel to heal after a few months of daily attention. However, before that sore healed another developed in the area where the diaper she wore at night touched her skin and where her thigh touched the edge of the wheelchair. One day, the pressure-sore nurse stopped coming to Grandaisy's room. The night nurse informed me that he had been fired.

"Why?"

The nurse shrugged, "Probably spending too much time with his patients."

Fortunately, Mom's long search for a new convalescent home paid off. She found one that was clean, bright, and lovingly staffed. However, by that time, Grandaisy had deteriorated significantly. She was getting most of her nutrition from a liquid food supplement, her weight was down to 120 pounds, and her muscle mass had atrophied far below the recommended one inch between skin and bone.

Grandaisy's skin was as thin and fragile as tissue paper. Her voice had grown so soft that speaking her thoughts audibly was difficult. Most noticeably, she stopped asking to come home. Still, she welcomed us with a bright smile.

Ultimately, a bone-deep and infected pressure sore caused gangrene to develop in her leg, so the doctor at the convalescent home sent Grandaisy to the hospital for an evaluation by a surgeon. After lifting the edge of the sheet that covered her leg, the surgeon announced he would have to amputate the limb to save her life.

"I need to do the operation. Will you have the surgery?"

Grandaisy looked him in the eye for a long second, then lengthened her spine and took a deep breath. "No!" she said in a strong, forceful voice.

"Then there's nothing I can do here," the surgeon said, looking at my mother before storming out of the room.

Grandaisy returned to the convalescent home where the nursing staff moved her into their acute care section. For the remaining months of her life, we were allowed to stay with her day and night. Friends, former foster children, and family came from all over the country to visit. A foster son in the Navy spent his leave at her bedside. Grandaisy focused her full attention on each visitor. She seemed to bathe people with love, drinking them in one final time.

At midnight, on December 8, 1998, during a full moon, Grandaisy's spirit peacefully rode the gusts of a windstorm to the place where her mother, sister, and Husband—the love of her life—lived. Her face wore a look of perfect peace. She was 95.

Six years later, in 2004, headlines worldwide proclaimed the death of "Superman" star Christopher Reeve. Nine years after becoming paralyzed, Reeve died of complications arising from an infected pressure sore. It happened quickly.

To me, Christopher Reeve was an inspiration and a hero. So was Grandaisy. No hero deserves the suffering the both of them had to endure.

By Kit Kirkpatrick

Kit Kirkpatrick holds a life teaching credential in English from the University of California, Davis, and a master of arts in communication studies from California State University, Sacramento.

She earned a living as a commercial writer producing press kits, feature stories, pitch letters and other marketing materials on behalf of her clients.

She previously edited and published a statewide magazine, *California Restaurateur*, and she has taught English as a Foreign Language at all grade levels.

She is currently enrolled in Pacifica University's Certified Memoirist Program, and she teaches the Memoirs Class through the UC Davis Extension.

Carrier
of Hemophilia

I am a carrier of hemophilia who was lucky enough to have a
healthy boy, a boy who is not a bleeder. I am the daughter of a
carrier; my chances of getting a healthy boy were 50-50. However,
my sisters and I were taught otherwise. In our mother's time, it
was thought that if a carrier had no sons, the line of this hereditary
disease—Bleeder's Disease it was once called—would come to a genetic
end. "We are so blessed with our four girls," Mom used to croon.
"Hemophilia ends with you."

In all, we four girls produced a total of five sons: three are bleeders and two are not.

My nephew Connor was the first to be diagnosed. He was born
three years after his healthy older brother, and 10 years after my son,
his healthy cousin Harry.

Connor's diagnosis was difficult and came only after a doctor
accused my sister Wanda of child abuse for Connor's repeated visits
to emergency. When the doctor asked about violence in the home,
I could imagine how Wanda's nose flared in anger. How dare he?
Then she clutched her baby to her in fear. They could file reports.
He wanted to take pictures. But Wanda's made of iron, thin but she
could be so cold. I imagine she went cold on that doctor that he
backed away.

"We want to know why he's getting these goose eggs every time
he falls. How will he learn to walk?" Wanda was scared and confused
because her baby wasn't bumping his head very hard. She didn't con-
sider hemophilia as a possible answer, because of course the disease
had ended with us. But when the doctor mumbled something about

how rare it is to discover hemophilia, Wanda's mind flashed. But how could it be? Hadn't our mother told us?

Thus began Wanda's own anguish and her abiding guilt for the defective human being her genes had created. My own heart sank when I'd heard her moan, "This is all my fault. He's just a boy."

Wanda never cried as she tried to keep her screaming toddler still for the IV needle, or when she kept a watchful eye on the playground with a cooler containing a $2000 vial of clotting factor and a needle, just in case. She cried in private, but always kept Connor blameless. "This is all my fault." My own heart bled, especially to see how she never let it go. I was among the many to counsel her to stop blaming herself, though I knew she had no ears for it.

The 50-50 chance of getting a healthy boy bore out in Wanda's case: two boys, one healthy and one a bleeder. But my sister Freya wasn't so lucky with her two boys were both bleeders, and by now we all knew of the risk.

I remember when Freya's first son, Nathan, was born. They were living in Menlo Park and Wanda had left Sacramento in time to be there for the birth, as though her presence might force a healthy boy to be born. But they knew at birth, from the umbilical blood, that Nathan was a "hemmie." Wanda went immediately into grief for our sister Freya. She couldn't congratulate Freya or say what-a-beautiful-baby boy. Wanda kept saying how sorry, how very very sorry, she was that Freya would have her fate.

"It's so hard," was Wanda's new mother advice, "I'm so sorry you'll have this life."

But Freya wasn't sorry. She was delighted and couldn't wait to teach her boy the gentle art of gardening, raising rabbits, swimming and even tennis. He was well-protected as a toddler and grew to be a man with relatively few emergency-room visits. Nathan is now married and will not have children. He's careful and once narrowly survived an emergency gall bladder removal.

Connor, on the other hand, felt cheated of a normal life. I think it's because his mother, Wanda, kept telling him that he had been cheated and it wasn't his fault. So, Connor had many more emergency room visits. He thought he deserved to play sports like basketball and baseball. A snowboarding injury led to a long hospitalization with a bleed into his hip that ultimately destroyed the joint. The hip damage occurred shortly before the "miracle" nasal spray came out. One $1000 squirt into the nostrils immediately after an injury and the new drug would clot anything that was bleeding internally—most of the time.

It is true that every baby boy has a 50-50 chance, but Freya figured her chances would be better with the next baby. First, it could be a girl and girls aren't bleeders (except when a bleeder marries a carrier, which has happened). And if it's a boy, then maybe the odds would be in her favor. But no. Her next baby was also a boy, and a bleeder. His name is James. Freya became more cautious with James. Besides, James saw his brother's care and emergency room visits before he learned to walk. He grew up knowing he couldn't take risks and backed away from life.

"Hey James," his father asked him when he started high school. "Is it better to have tried and failed, or never to have tried at all?"

"No brainer, Dad! Better not to try." He doesn't plan to have children.

Connor, on the other hand, is married and has two daughters, both full carriers. Those girls, if they have boys, will have boys who are certain bleeders. Connor's daughters will have to make the decision their father did not: do I want a part in furthering this disease?

What decision would I have made if I'd known?

Thank you, Mom, for the misinformation that allowed me to be free and to adore my son without guilt. I was so lucky.

By Adele Tarantino

Adele Tarantino, who usually writes under the pen name of Adele Lawrence, is a retired teacher.

She has enjoyed working in various schools on the San Francisco Peninsula—from elementary through adult education.

With a bachelor's degree in education and a master's in sociology, her interests are as widely varied as her writing.

"I've been long-time editor of a newsletter promoting opportunities for women and girls," she says. "My ultimate joy was teaching a memoir writing class for seniors. My Life's theme: Write On!"

Nowhere, Nevada

D ad pulled our Jeep SUV into the small gas station. We were almost out of gas and had to get off the main road to refill if we wanted to get home. We were going home from a vacation in Reno where we saw the famous air show they have every year. Thunder and lightning were striking every five minutes. Mom sat nervously in the front seat. My friend Ryan and I sat in the back seat playing our Gameboys.

A strange-looking old man struggled out of the gas-station office to help us. "You ain't goin' nowhere in this storm," he said. "If I were you, I'd stay at the motel down the road."

"Where are we?" Mom asked as she looked at the map in her lap.

"You're in Nowhere, Nevada," said the old man. "And we ain't goin' nowhere. Haven't been since the silver mine shut down back in 1894."

"Thanks," said Dad as he paid the man and grumbled to Mom about what a way to end a vacation.

The wind nearly blew us off the narrow road, but we finally spotted the lights of the motel.

"Do we have to stay here, Dad?" I asked, thinking about dirty beds and rats waiting for us. And who knows what else!

"No choice," said Dad, and he went into the office to rent our room. Ryan looked as scared as I felt when we got out of the car and went toward our room in the back of the motel where we were going to spend the night.

Mom and Dad went to sleep right away, but Ryan and I lay there talking when suddenly we heard a whispering voice, "Go away, go away, go away." It was coming from the closet. We opened the door, and it was empty, but then we saw a smaller door at the back of the dirty closet.

"How strange," said Ryan as he turned the doorknob.

"I don't like this at all," I said, and then we saw stairs that led down into darkness.

"Let's give it a try," said Ryan.

We were feeling cold in our light pajamas but were curious to know where the stairs were going. We had a flashlight in the car, so I ran to get it and we started to explore.

We shined the flashlight and jumped back when we saw a skeleton at the bottom of the stairs, lying against the wall of what looked like an underground cave.

"Look what's in his hand," I whispered. We crept closer and I grabbed the rolled-up piece of paper; the skeleton's hand fell off. We yelled and backed away but then shined the flashlight on the paper. It was a map. On the top was faded writing that said, "Old Ben's Silver Mine"

"I guess that's Old Ben," Ryan said. We decided to call what was a small hole, Old Ben.

"Why not take a look," I said. Ryan followed me as I crawled through the hole. We found ourselves in another cave, even larger than the one Old Ben's skeleton was in. There were pickaxes and shovels and pails laying around on the ground and the air was hard to breathe.

A loud bang and rumble reminded us of the storm going on above us. Then our flashlight shined on the face of a man—or was it really a man? The face was white, the eyes black, and the hair looked like someone had plugged him into an electric socket. It stuck out all over.

"You'll never have my mine!" he roared. "I may be dead, but no one will have Old Ben's silver. Now get out of here you nosey kids."

"You got it, mister." I shouted back. Ryan and I turned fast and crawled back through the hole. We waved our hands at the skeleton and raced back up the stairs to the safety of our motel room. We were both sweating.

We jumped into our beds and were shaking like leaves. Dad and Mom woke up when we slammed the closet door.

"What happened?" asked Dad. We told them our story, but they just laughed and said the dark and stormy night was making us imagine things.

"Oh no, Mom," I cried. Just look in the closet but don't open that little door!" Well, Mom looked in the closet and what she saw was some old clothes hanging there and on the floor was a miner's hat, and a rusty pickax and shovel. Ryan and I couldn't believe our eyes. No door? No stairs? No skeleton? No map? No ghost of Old Ben? How could that be?

The storm was over. Dad and Mom dressed and told us to get in the car.

"We're not staying here any longer," Dad said. "I'll drive all night if I have to. This place is nowhere I want to be."

"Us either, Dad," I said as I looked at Ryan. Ryan agreed with me. We were feeling lucky because we had escaped the angry ghost of Old Ben. "We're never gonna' forget this haunted motel and the town called Nowhere, Nevada," I told Dad.

The Jeep headed towards home and safety.

By Brina Patel

Brina Patel graduated from the University of California, Santa Barbara, with a bachelor's degree in psychology and an education minor.

She enjoys writing pieces that involve humor, anecdotes from her travels, and insight into cultural experiences.

Her goal is to write and publish a memoir that recounts her seven-month sojourn in India after her college graduation.

She is currently a freelance writer. Her website is www.brinapatelwriter.com and she can be reached at brina@brinapatelwriter.com.

Dropping the Shield

The midmorning sun streamed through the kitchen window like a spotlight. I bathed in its warm glow as I listened to my grandmothers' high-pitched chatter, which ricocheted off the walls around us. The women compared recipes for *magaj*, a Gujarati delicacy, debating the correct *ghee*-to-sugar ratio. I leaned against the beige tiled countertop and watched my paternal grandmother knead the *roti* dough, her hands pulsating like a beating heart. The *pallu* of her teal *sari* slipped off her shoulder, and she paused to reposition it. My maternal grandmother had her back to us. Her hair was pulled into a loose braid, clasped together by a golden pin. She stirred the *dal* and *shaak* that occupied the rear two burners of the stove, stopping to taste test one of them before adding an extra dash of salt. The tight kitchen filled with the dishes' aromas—bearing hints of garlic, onion, cumin—and my mouth began to water.

I could hear the faint chatter of my dad and grandfathers in the living room, though much of it was inaudible through the steady hum of the stove fan. My mom was out running last-minute errands for the guests who would be arriving within the next hour. I fetched the wooden rolling pin and board from their designated drawer, as my paternal grandmother placed a bowl with round balls of dough in front of me. Though I was only nine, I was already familiar with the process. I dipped a ball in flour, the ashy texture of the granules making my hands feel like chalk and began to roll.

"When you live with your in-laws," my paternal grandmother said in Gujarati as she watched me churn out a lopsided *roti*. "They'll expect your cooking to be *superb*."

I feigned a smile and stepped aside so she could fix my creation, then reached for another dough ball.

"Before we start planning her marriage," my maternal grandmother chimed in, "we must first make sure she becomes a top-notch doctor."

The women shared a laugh and carried on their conversation. But in that moment, I froze, my mind zoned out as I continued rolling mechanically.

I was bombarded by that word from as early as I could remember. Each time I heard it my mouth dried up like a ball of cotton. Eight letters. One merciless punch to the gut. *Marriage.*

Images would conjure up in my head. The most prevalent was one of myself in a red and gold *sari*. A garland of fresh marigolds was strung around my neck while my hands and feet were decorated by elaborate *mehndi* designs. I looked into the face of my future self for a sign of reassurance. All I wanted was a smile or a twinkle in someone's eye to reassure me that my fears were unwarranted. Yet all I could see was a girl with a downcast gaze and a sunken face. Perhaps the futuristic self of my imagination wasn't me, but an avatar of all the women before me.

I'm the child of first-generation immigrants. My father hails from the farmlands of western India and my mother from the Midlands of England, though she is Indian in origin. Both sides of my family relocated to the U.S. in the mid-1980s. The promise of greater opportunities was one too enticing to pass up.

Though they had to adapt to life in the U.S. in a physical sense— driving on the opposite side of the road, for instance— they remained steadfast in their traditions.

Things in my family had always been run according to age-old customs, particularly regarding gender roles. A woman was expected to move in with her husband and his parents after marriage. Her duties centered around caretaking and homemaking. A man was the *de facto* breadwinner.

As a child of the 1990s and early 2000s, I sat at the cusp of a generational struggle. There was a tug-of-war between the old ways and the new. From about the age of eight or nine, I was being primed for marriage. My aunts and grandmothers made it their mission to ensure that I'd learn to prepare perfect *chai* and the roundest *rotis*, qualities which would be sure to impress my future mother-in-law. In addition to this, I was also expected to be at the top of my class and enter a "respected" profession like medicine or business. This would give me an edge above the other girls when my "time came."

My grandmothers had both been pulled from school before the

age of ten. Education was seen as a frivolous pursuit for girls who would be married by their eighteenth birthdays. For women of their generation and generations prior, marriage was not something that carried any semblance of choice. It was a carefully calculated transaction. Caste, astrological factors, and family reputation were considered when pairing young bachelors and bachelorettes. Marriage was not so much a woman and man tying the knot, but one extended family marrying the other.

For my parents' generation, arranged marriages were still, by and large, the norm. Yet there was a small but increasing number of converts to a new option—the *love* marriage. Those with love marriages were seen as anomalies. Everyone was either jealous of the couples who pursued one or placed bets on their eventual demise. Though perhaps the latter group was more envious.

By the time I entered high school, I was enveloped in dissonance. On the one hand, I possessed a deep pride in my culture and my Indian roots. But on the other, I felt as if they'd left me confined. To the outside world, I was putting on a façade as "the good Indian girl." The one who would say "yes" to the best boy my elders found and study her way into medical school. But on the inside, I was merely a puppet strung along at the will of others.

At home, there was a looming expectation to stay within the predetermined boundaries when it came to my career trajectory and future partner. There was a sense of fear instilled in me to do otherwise, particularly when it came to marrying interracially or, god forbid, to someone of a different religion. The brave souls in our extended network who did take this step were ostracized or if they were lucky heavily ridiculed.

"You know so-and-so's daughter? She married the American man. Such a shame," I'd hear older relatives say, shaking their heads as if the girl had been consumed by flesh-eating bacteria.

I couldn't help but wonder if there was something to it. If these love marriages—which often transcended race, caste, religion— were all that bad. I'd seen the way "regular" couples behaved—walking hand-in-hand, giggling as they gazed into one another's eyes. My best friend Sandy's parents seemed to be pulling it off. My neighbors, too. Heck, even celebrities were doing it.

But I couldn't shake the anxiety. A love marriage was a gamble, as far as I'd learned. And I believed I should respect my elders' wishes and find someone to their liking. No matter how hard I tried, though, I couldn't block out the whispering of an altogether different narrative, its breath warm in my ear. *Follow your heart.*

Once I entered college, I was like a child being introduced to junk food for the first time. Freedom and choice were at my disposal, sitting and waiting for me to take advantage of all they had to offer. I chose to major in the topic that most interested me (psychology) and dressed however I so pleased (enough short skirts and tank tops to make my grandmothers faint).

Living five hours from home and in an environment full of young men my age, I also got to do something many of my non-Indian friends had been doing for years: date.

I made a vow to myself that I'd marry a non-Indian man just to defy my family and the very notion of an arranged marriage. Every boy I dated was more out of spite to my upbringing than out of factors such as compatibility, or genuine attraction. Truth be told, I didn't even know what *my* interests were. Or who *I* was. This one-sided dating, however, led to an emotional avalanche, with either my feelings or the feelings of the other person being crushed. Needless to say, my idea of a relationship was warped.

I decided to delay the 9-to-5 world after graduation and instead go on a pilgrimage of sorts back to my motherland. *Maybe I'll finally understand a bit more about the whole marriage mumbo jumbo,* I told myself.

What I didn't expect was the rise of a wave of repressed anger which had been boiling beneath the surface for over twenty years. *How could my family be so narrow-minded?* I thought to myself. I felt deprived. My fists clenched with rage on behalf of all the other Indian girls who didn't have the ability to make their own decisions.

I saw young Indian girls who reminded me of myself, timid and afraid. I saw girls my age who were mothers, or who'd recently been married. And I couldn't help but think of how different my fate would have been had my family never left India.

I was also surprised to see, though, more women than I expected who were single. Not just younger ones, but women who were in their early thirties, or even older. Many had also had love marriages in defiance of their family's protests. Some were divorced. I struggled to make sense of it all.

I spent a month in Goa, a beachside state in western India. Goa was known for its laid-back atmosphere in comparison to the rest of the country's chaos. It was there I befriended Priya, a Nepali artist who was thirty-four and unmarried. She emanated an assuredness in herself that I hadn't before witnessed in a South Asian woman. Her posture was open and unguarded, as if she possessed no need to shield herself from the world. And her hair was shorn just above her shoulders, while her arms bore tattoos. Though Priya was content in her career and social life, her family didn't believe she would be "whole" unless she found a suitor.

It was a breezy day and we sat in a café nestled along the Arabian Sea, the waves choppy while the sun shone high in the sky. As Priya and I chatted, I noticed, though oceans apart from one another, we had been socialized with the same rigid expectations. We had the same fears and points of frustration. She, as well, had had her own rebellion of sorts, going through a phase of partying and boyfriend hopping in her early 20s.

"How do you deal with all of these pressures to marry?" I asked Priya in exasperation.

"Well, perhaps it's not so much the thought of marriage itself," she said. "But the fact that our generation is the first to defy these millennia-long practices, the first generation to openly question them. I think there is a lot of weight in that."

The tension in my shoulders released as her words sunk in.

"We feel liberated," Priya carried on. "But we also feel afraid of this unknown terrain, one we have to carve out for ourselves. We want to be happy, but we also don't want to hurt our elders. Or lose their love. It's all so new for us. And it's hard."

She also talked about her guilt; guilt over the sacrifices her family had made so she could get an education and pursue her dreams. And I felt as if that was why I was so hung up on it all, too. Because of my family's hard work and strife, I'd felt an indebtedness to them. An inner fight between my own needs and theirs.

As the evening rolled in, I stared out at the waves before me, their crests now undulating in a gentler manner as the sun began to set, casting a golden hue upon the waters. My mind and body possessed a lightness that I'd never felt. Priya's words allowed me to see things from a zoomed-out perspective. It was the first time I'd viewed the arranged marriage situation for what it was, from the other stance, and a more objective one. My parents, grandparents, and the generations before had made immense sacrifices so that mine could enjoy a higher quality of life. The marital traditions were their way of preserving what had the potential to become defunct. They were afraid of letting us out into the unknown, of making mistakes and shattering the images and bonds they had worked so hard to obtain. But it was my generation's chance to break cycles and to hold on to what did serve us and release what no longer did.

Now, as I enter my late 20s— the prime time for getting hitched as seen in my friend circles— I feel myself move toward forgiveness. I can better view the customs for what they are and appreciate my family's journey and history. Many of them have accepted the generational shift toward autonomy, while others still attain a more purist mindset. Though it is often difficult, I try to remind myself that neither side is necessarily "right." But I do hope more young South Asians will have the privilege of choice that myself and many in my generation do now.

I reimagine the woman I'd think of as a child; the one on her wedding day. There are multiple versions of her. In some fantasies, she is adorned in a white wedding gown, and in others an embellished *sari*. In some she stands amid evergreens on a balmy day, in others she sits atop a traditional *mandap*, illuminated by bright fluorescent lights. In some, she is a few days shy of her thirtieth, in others she is pushing forty. However, in each of them, there's no doubting the twinkle in her eye and the smile on her face. She appears in control of her fate.

Marriage is not something I want to detest or fear. I want to be its ally. And I feel this, as I've dropped the shield that covered me for so long. There's no longer an urge to fight, freeze, or flee the concept of marriage. But a desire to embrace it like a long-lost friend.

Torian Taylor Kathleen *(decorative vertical title)*

By Kathleen Torian Taylor

Kathleen Torian Taylor earned a bachelor of arts degree in drama and dance from the University of the Pacific in Stockton, California.

She is a retired professional dancer, choreographer, and teacher. She received the Outstanding Achievement Award in Dance from the Stockton Arts Commission and was granted the California State Legislature Certificate of Recognition.

The author joined the Grossenbacher's Elk Grove Writers & Artists group in 2013. Her novella, *Death by Arrangement*, was published in February 2021.

She is also a working poet. Four of her poems have been published in the 2020 Redwood Writers anthology.

Death by Arrangement

June 2014, Lake Malibu

H e let the car roll down the hill and listened to the dry crunch of branches under the tires. The car slowed into a large grove of trees far from the camping area. At 11:00 p.m. Lake Malibu lit up with the full moon's silver reflections. He pressed the window button and the glass slid down. After he turned off the engine, the cool air and the aroma of pine jumpstarted his energy, as it always had.

He fingered the knife in his pocket and took in the scattered picnic tables and pines. There was the perfect tree by the lake. He used to play a game there, dividing the space between soldiers, good and bad. He'd stand on the good table, holding a sword he made from a branch and yell his command, "Surrender or die!" Since Mother was his only audience, she'd cheer as he won the battle.

He scanned the view of the water and what was once their vacation home cradled within the Santa Monica Mountains.

Mother, remember the ghost story about the Lady of the Lake? I was sure she would drag me out of bed and plunge me into her dark world. And the old movies they'd show at night, Mother, so many of them. "How Green Was My Valley," "Mr. Blandings Builds His Dream House." We'd devour a box of chocolate-covered cherries.

A branch crackled and he grabbed his chest. A deer paused in front of the car. Only a doe. They shared a quiet moment and then she evaporated into the brush.

He wrapped his hands around the leather steering wheel and lowered his forehead onto its forgiving softness. He could smell those hamburgers sizzling on an old black cast iron pan as he and Mother huddled together by the campfire. They melted chocolate bars and marshmallows crushed between graham crackers. She applied white cream on his nose so it wouldn't burn. They'd drift for hours in their paddleboat. The wind would lift her dark, shoulder-length hair. She always had a sheer red scarf tied around her neck—her signature piece of clothing—along with her cardigan sweater and pleated skirt. Mother had deep brown eyes that spoke to you

without words.

Enough of walking through the past. He popped open the glove compartment and took out a plastic bag filled with chopped heads of lavender. He gathered a few and squeezed them between his fingers. Mother's scent filled the air. He retrieved the small box of chocolate-covered cherries—Mother's favorite—and placed them inside with the lavender.

Time to finish up. As he rubbed his hands together, adrenaline surged through him with the force of a waterfall. He looked over his shoulder to make sure no campers had come up behind him. After releasing the trunk, he stepped out of the car. In the distance a dog barked, and he ducked. The sound drifted into silence.

After digging into his coat pocket, he removed a pair of latex gloves, tugged them onto his hands, and snapped them at the wrists. What a long day. Things needed to be tidied up. He made one last inspection to make sure no late-night campers were out for an evening jaunt, then headed for the rear of the car. The trunk stood halfway open. His hand slid along the cold metal. He pushed the lid and it drifted up, revealing its contents.

He gazed down at her. She was dressed in a pleated skirt and cardigan sweater. *There you are my latest triumph. You look as if you decided to curl up and take a nap.* He laughed a little at the duct tape across her mouth. *You no longer need that, do you?*

He ducked his head under the lid. *You're staring up at me.* He closed her eyelids and noted rigor mortis had not yet set in. Her skin had turned an ashen color. He peeled the tape off her mouth, then took the knife from his jacket pocket and cut the rope binding her hands and ankles. *You're so petite, probably don't weigh more than a hundred pounds.* Removing her from the trunk was not as easy as he'd imagined. Her body was already stiffening.

He concentrated on the lake and spotted the perfect tree. As he lowered her against its trunk, he momentarily lost his balance. She slipped through his fingers like some discarded bag of trash. *I'm sorry, Theresa. Mother always scolded me for being so awkward.* Her skirt rode up her thighs. Pinching his lips and swearing under his breath, he nudged her until she was positioned against the coarse bark. When he heard a twig snap, he fell to his side. Only a squirrel. He watched it dart up a tree, and his nerves electrified. *Hurry up.*

Time to get his arrangements underway. He always dressed his girls in the proper attire, and he was especially proud of this one. He stretched out her legs and removed the shoes. They would be added to his collection. He crossed her ankles and folded her hands across her lap. He made sure the pleated skirt covered her knees, and he buttoned the top of her cardigan sweater.

Theresa, I told you the evening would be exciting. If only I had someone to share my accomplishment with. Someone who'd appreciate the effort that goes into my creative process.

After removing a comb from his pocket, he parted her hair down the middle, then flicked away a few pine needles that drifted onto her arm. Her soft brown waves touched her shoulders. Pulling back her bangs to the right, he clipped on a tortoise-shell barrette to complete the look. He applied deep red lipstick to her lips, retrieved a red sheer scarf from his pants pocket, smoothed out its wrinkles, and tied the scarf around her neck.

There, that hides those nasty bruises. Kneeling beside her, he turned to face the lake. You have a perfect view. I wish we could've spent more time talking about your art exhibit. Not the greatest, but your work probably attracted tourists. He took one last look at the lake and then back at her. There was such purity about her posed against the tree.

Have to leave now. He ran his hand down one side of her hair, smoothing a couple of uncooperative strands. *Goodbye.* He slid the box of chocolates from the plastic bag and placed it on her lap. He removed some of the lavender, rubbed the purple heads behind her cars and the soft veins of her wrists.

He rose and took another look to make sure no one was heading his way. *Must be almost midnight.*

He ambled back to the car, kicking small pinecones from his path. Just another guy out for a stroll. Glancing down he noticed a thin layer of dust on his new Italian leather shoes. Mother would not approve of dirty loafers. *Hmmm. Time for a shoeshine.*

By Frederick Foote

Native Sacramentan Frederick Foote writes short stories, essays, and poetry.

He has published more than 360 articles. His portfolio includes three collections of short stories: *For the Sake of Soul, Crossroads Encounters* and *The Maroon: Fables and Revelations.*

Foote is known for packing in the crowds at readings, to the delight of those lucky enough to be in attendance. He has also spoken at numerous writing and community events.

Frederick Foote

Our Sister Koss

You know what's bad? When people talk about you behind your back and put your name all over the street. *That's* bad.

Do you know what's worse? When people know, on some unconscious level, that it would be dangerous business to talk bad about you—to *anyone*. It's not that these people dislike, hate, despise, or fear you. Their feelings are deeper than that. So deep that they don't want to understand why they feel the way they do.

Don't look at me like that. I'm not talking about me. I'm talking about our sister.

Not June. My older sister, June, is fifteen and a full-on nerd with an attitude. I like being around her sometimes. She's always the star of her own show.

I'm talking about my eight-year-old sister, Koss.

By the way, my name is Klein, and I'm twelve years old. I'm not as smart or as outgoing as June. I'm more of a loner. I like to take my time and feel my way through things.

Koss is eight and looks like an average Black girl with braces and bangs and silly giggles.

But June and I, and our parents, know that this is just a kind of disguise. Koss is our sister, but she is a whole lot more than that. I mean, it's like the sister part of her is the tip of the iceberg that looks nothing like the part of her you can't see.

Koss is a boy's or girl's name that has been in our family for so long that nobody knows its origin anymore.

So, one reason we believe Koss is way more than she appears to be is that she will freeze up for a few seconds—or minutes sometimes.

We're convinced that she's traveling in her other body during those spells. We believe this because we've asked Koss, and she has described some of the places she visits—places with lakes of melted greed like hydrochloric acid eating away at every living thing and turning the air into poison. But there are things that thrive in the lake. They look a lot like us but with gates for mouths and picket-fence fangs. It's a place where there is blackness so thick you can taste it. There is no ground or sky or up or down. There are screams of dying, tortured, terrified, things coming at random from every direction forever. Her Koss body could not have survived the places she visited.

When Koss was five, I asked her how old she really was. She smiled at me, touched my forehead with her finger, and whispered, "Klein, I don't know. I don't even understand that question." She giggled, pushed back her bangs, and went to search the freezer for ice cream for us.

I like hanging out with Koss more than June. I kind of know what's happening with June, and that gets old. However, with Koss, there is the feeling that anything and everything can happen in the blink of an eye. I don't know quite how to describe the way I feel. I guess it's kind of like holding your breath waiting for the end of the world, or the beginning of the world, or something amazing like that.

June is not a Koss fan. She feels like Koss is stealing the spotlight from her. But when it is only the two of them, they seem to get along just fine.

Most of the time, I prefer to be by myself. I like reading, drawing, and playing video games.

Sometimes, I just need to be near Mom or Dad, and I will sit by them. They always welcome me. It's like they need to be with me, too.

Last year, in the last week of school, Odell Woods, a boy I have known for years, came up to me during morning recess.

Koss was in the weedy part of the playground trying to catch "hopper grasses." That's what Koss called grasshoppers. For some reason, my sister could never grasp the word grasshopper.

This was the first time I really understood how people felt about Koss. It was like everybody on the playground was a herd of wildebeest on the African plain. And they all knew a lion was watching them. And they knew the lion was not after them, but all eyes were on the lion. Their lives depended on knowing where the lion was at all times. I mean, no one was looking at or staring at Koss, but everyone was aware of where she was.

It was a very tense moment. It was as if the herd had elected Odell to represent them. Odell stopped about six feet from me, took a deep breath, and spoke. "Klein, is Koss an angel?"

Koss was leaping to catch a hopper grass.

Everyone on the playground was waiting, breathless, for my reply.

The question caught Koss's attention for just a split second.

The playground herd felt Koss glance at them and was on the verge of panic and stampede.

I said, "No. Why would you even think that?"

Odell was sweating like a melting popsicle on a hundred-degree day. He took two steps back, turned around, and walked off the playground and out of the schoolyard. No one tried to stop him. I never saw Odell again.

I looked at the people around Koss more closely after that. People watched her out of the corners of their eyes. They never, never let their eyes linger on Koss or stare at her. And I could almost hear the sigh of relief when Koss left the area.

I looked at how people treated me and June because of Koss. We didn't have any real friends. I mean, people went *way* out of their way not to offend us. But no one wanted to get too close. I guess that's how people treat the children of gangsters and tyrants.

I talked to June about this, and she agreed with me. She said she stopped caring about what people thought when she was about my age. June said living with Koss was like living on the slope of a volcano. "You know it's just a matter of time until BOOM!" I never felt like that. That was a really sad conversation.

Koss and I were playing Monopoly at our kitchen table.

"Koss, are you, like, watching all the people, grading them, trying to decide what to do with us?" Before she could respond, I asked, "Do you even know *what* you are?"

Koss moved her top hat four spaces to Go.

She grabbed my hand and held it tight as she spoke, "I'm not a judgment machine, silly. I know that one day you will see me—the *real* me. Let me know what you see, okay?"

"It'll be too late then," I said without thinking, but I know it was the truth.

Koss did too. She stood and left the kitchen. She needed to be alone.

I went and squeezed in between Mom and Dad on the couch. They were watching some old black-and-white western.

June came and sat with us.

It was a tight fit, but it felt right.

Eventually, Koss spoke to us, and everyone everywhere, "It won't be long now. Just close your eyes and look at me. You can look at me now."
    We did.

By Ted Witt

Ted Witt is the publisher behind Pretty Road Press, an independent publishing company in Folsom, California, where he specializes in content syndication and trade books.

He previously served as vice president of CWC's Sacramento Writers, where he emphasized that marketing skills are as important for today's authors as writing skills.

He is a former newspaper reporter from San Diego County and California's Central Coast.

He later transitioned to public relations and lobbying in the education arena in Sacramento before taking the job as executive director of the California Association of School Business Officials. He then became the vice president of a private Bay Area firm specializing in software and consulting for schools.

He is the author of the business book, *No One Ever Told Me That*. His bylines top scores of newspaper, magazine, and website articles.

The Oaks

Fresh into the infant autumn, the oaks, early in their preparation for winter, have begun to drop their leaves. They started their preparation several weeks ago when August issued its orders: "All acorns to the ground." Today, nature's morning recarpeting reminds me of the seasonality of life—a clarion sign of what awaits me.

A greater number of leaves will fall as the evenings make a play for power and grab the light. Daylight will subside; darkness will exaggerate the moon. The contest is a prelude to honking geese swiftly making their way south. They will travel in great numbers as November approaches. Still, if history repeats itself, a solitary early bird will honk his way past my bedroom window at the crack of dawn. I will watch him through the naked branches of an oak framing his silhouette.

Each fall weekend I venture out alongside the edges of my oak branches with a noisy lawnmower, leveling the blades of grass to an even plane. Afterward, the greens announce their teamwork, every blade erect as though dressed in an emerald uniform properly starched.

Though I wish each culm would grow equally in height, nature reminds me that each will mature separately above the soil it's given. The mulching of fall's contribution offers no equal opportunity, only a home for each seedling's similar effort. My mower comes along and promises the appearance of equality for each, but it is only an illusion.

I contrast my lawn with today's online viewing of the wild meadows of Yosemite. The grass, though brown, looks more beautiful than my lawn. Its stalks of random heights wave in the breeze. Rain will come soon, and the Yosemite fields will turn green. Streams will quicken.

Snow will caulk the cracks and corners of the granite cliffs—unmovable no matter what the season.

Each autumn of my life, nature's pattern has repeated itself with certainty. I know nature will be faithful to its appointed destiny this year, even though I worry my neglect, or my intrusions, may harm my oaks. I estimate them to be at least a century old. I fear I will unknowingly over-water the nearby lawn or give a blind eye to the holes of a pesky wood-pecker. Fortunately, the oaks are robust and craftier than I am, thriving in a way my bones cannot compete.

Last year's pelting of acorns left dozens of seedlings. I am surprised how many have survived the spring and summer in my front yard. It seems the oaks' sole job each season is to dress the fertile loam beneath its branches with baby oaks. Scores of tiny, deeply rooted twigs attest to the mother trees' success.

However, the world is harsh. Death hovers. Few, if any, of these skinny twigs will find their way to arboreal adolescence. In spite of the opportunities afforded them by one hundred seasons, only three oaks stand in my yard, the mothers themselves. Occasionally, their maternal joints will creak in a strong wind, but I never hear them mourning over their solitude. I only see obedience to their calling—more acorns in each season.

All around me, the world turns in mathematical balance, prompting a personal reflection on the seasons of my life. I'm sure I have entered a new season because I have budding questions: Have I properly pruned the world around me? Did I graft for mere appearance or for a more robust stalk? Yes, I gratefully appreciate the grand mission of the speed-ing goose, but did I prepare for my own winters properly? Could I have saved more seedlings and fostered more nests?

My own acorn offspring have sprouted into tall and sprightly oaks. Did I prepare them for life's boring beetles?

My mind's priorities are called up for review. I see the past in dif-ferent colors. I perceive time differently. The future seems shorter. I frequently wonder what will grow under my branches when they no longer flower.

My thoughts are no cause for alarm. They are as mundane as autumn's dirt. Many more and wiser men than I have pondered greater, deeper, and broader into nature and our human existence. In fact, some have contemplated too long and missed the obvious: Oaks exist to make new oaks, to feed the squirrels, to nest the birds, to shade the weary, to supply the carpenter, and, perhaps most important, to testify to the poetic order of life.

Yes, there is order, a universal message that answers my persistent questions. "Stand tall like me," shouts the oak. "Nurture seedlings with your branches. Shelter the homeless owl. Build with my wood. Grow a strong trunk. Support branches that point to the sky. Look up like me. Be proud and shout your silent messages of strength and hope and reason."

Now night has fallen. The wind has picked up. I hear the mother oaks creaking again. Their remaining leaves canter and parade toward earth for no audience, save me with my meditations of the season's rhythmic lessons of obedience.

POETRY

By Gloria Pierrot-Dyer

Gloria Pierrot-Dyer is a teacher and free-lance editor, holding degrees in Spanish and education as well as teaching credentials in elementary education and reading/language arts.

Her first book, *Allensworth: Two Tales of Triumph,* is set in the tiny, originally all-black town of Allensworth (now a part of the California State Parks system) where she grew up and attended its two-room school.

A delighted mother, grandmother, worship leader, and soloist, Gloria also enjoys reading, painting, travel, and studying foreign languages.

She is honored to serve on the CWC Sacramento Board of Directors.

I Put My
Troubles in a Jar

I put my troubles in a jar,
And screwed the lid on tight.
Each broken dream, each wounding word,
I put out of my sight.

Each failure I'd had to live with,
Regrets of every kind,
I stowed away within this jar
And put them out of mind.

And then I sought a secret place
To hide it from myself:
The darkest and remotest corner
Of the highest, unused shelf.

And there I left it with a smile,
And went on with my life.
With resolute, feigned serenity,
I quelled each hint of strife.

But one day without warning,
As I quietly sipped sweet tea,
With well-connected, soft-voiced friends,
Making small talk tranquilly.

There was a loud explosion,
A tremendous, earth-shattering blast
That rattled every teacup
And left us all aghast.

I hurried to my closet,
This noise to investigate,
Certain that whatever had fallen and made a mess,
Could be quickly cleared away.

But all was as I'd left it,
Neat and orderly.
'Twas then I finally realized
That the e x p l o s i o n
Had been
Me.

By JoAnn Anglin

One morning each week, JoAnn Anglin travels 20 miles to the "castle on the hill." Wearing appropriate clothes, she leaves behind any forbidden item. In her tote, she carries lesson plans, prepared for two classes of eight to 10 students. Every lesson she assigns is one she herself does, whether as homework or an in-class writing exercise.

A respected figure in the media field for many years and a practicing poet for more than 25, JoAnn teaches poetry at Folsom State Prison.

Waving off skeptics and naysayers, JoAnn remains committed to this calling after six years, during which she has come to learn the value of this extraordinary time, not just for her inmate students, but also for herself as a writer, an artist, and a person.

JoAnn published her first chapbook of poems, *Words Like Knives, Like Feathers*, three years ago through Rattlesnake Press. Her poems have also appeared in *100 Poems about Sacramento*, the *Anthology of the Third Sunday Poets*, the *Pagan Muse, Poems of Resistance, Voces del Nuevo Sol, Poetry Now*, and *The Los Angeles Review*.

Departs

She leaves in red high heel shoes

a flamenco of recriminations
hard hard sounds jolting the floor
and his brain tapering to softening
tap taps that draw the ear to turn
sideways to lean into the going.

She leaves in a twirl of hips
hands spinning with flourish her
words bounced against the sofa up to
the ceiling fan dribbling into corners,
trailing behind like a silk sash
come undone.

She leaves in a poison green '59 Cadillac
(the Reverse does not work) steering
wheel hand pulling hard right hard
left spraying a bar of radiance through
the single pane window – a three-second
sunrise/sunset on the wall.

She leaves back angry sorrow that clings
like a cloud of down left from the
eviscerated nestling fluff that caresses
holds fast and reappears over time in his
hair in the creases of his joints stuck
to his wondering heart.

By Loy Holder

Loy Holder's dream of becoming a writer got interrupted when cancer slowed her down, but her efforts came to fruition when she finally published her novel *Dancing Up the Ladder*.

When she formerly served as a California information technology project manager, she was a closet writer of poetry to those she loved – family, and special people in her life. But, she says, "I always dreamed of writing a book."

Throughout the challenging process of writing, publishing and marketing, she saw a need for affordable and easy access to a writer's conference in her local community.

So she became the project manager for the Elk Grove Writer's Conference. She chairs the Elk Grove Writers Guild and hosts weekly meetings of the Elk Grove Senior Center Writing Group—all while working on a second book.

Regrets

If I had a chance to do it again,
I'd take her to Weinstocks to browse within.
I'd take her to the Rosemont and wait patiently,
While she finished her meal and complained constantly.
I'd go to her house and sit for hours,
no matter her eyes should close.
I'd read her a book, or bring her some flowers
just to make sure she knows ...
I'd come no matter the times she lied
that she needed a doctor and wanted a ride.
I'd tell her she's pretty, and hope for a grin.
If I had a chance to do it again.

By Andrew Laufer

Andrew Laufer retired after a 25-year career with the California Department of Education.

He is currently a gentleman farmer, story-teller, poet, and author.

His recently published book *Papa Laufer's Stories: Positive reflections of life in America*, is a collection of single-page vignettes describing his life experiences.

These stories will make you laugh, and they will make you cry. They will make you think about life, and they will elicit similar memories of your own. A few are sad, most are humorous, all are thought provoking to either lighten your heart, or to move you to deeper conversations.

Giving Words

I pour out my soul
  in poetic verse
A means of sharing my life
My confidence sometimes waivers
  not because of my word
     but the uncertainty of understanding

 If you hear what I say
  it is a small gift to you
If you do not receive it
  my clarity comes into question
    as does your ability to listen
      or perhaps desire is absent

When the line includes controversy
  perspectives overwhelm
Divergent meanings often apply
  intentions that do not belong to me
Angst creeps into my mind
  when my failure, or yours, distort my meaning

My poetry is derived from genuine feelings
You are not required to agree
You may not want
  the gift I have to offer
but offer it I shall
  for it is mine to give

Your reaction is poetic too
Your intention unknown to me
I want to accept the gift you are sharing
    hoping I understand your meaning
Clarity will only come
    with the giving

By Eric Wiesenthal

Eric Wiesenthal is a native New Yorker and holds a bachelor's degree in print journalism from The American University in Washington, D.C.

He was a newspaper reporter for five years, including Capitol Hill. In Sacramento, he served in the state Assembly as a legislative aide and press secretary to one of the LatinX members.

He has been writing poetry and short stories for the last three years.

Detroit vs. Everybody

We're not "The City of Big Shoulders,"
but we've been "The Motor City," "Motown,"
and much more.

Built by
Greeks,
Germans
Irish, and
Poles and
Black folk of the Great Migration.

An engine for our nation.

Chevrolet, Chrysler, and Ford, to name a few,
pushing us forward anew
into the age of
speed and mass production.

So much power and life,

But none so huge as
River Rouge – Ford's colossus.

100,000 workers – a city,
its own steel mill
and the gritty work of many hands
from the docks to the line – hundreds of cars at one time.
And then came World War II,
bombers and tanks built by the slew.

When it was over,
Thunderbirds and Mustangs
roared forth – the stars.
And once again it was the cars
that powered this great city.

Then came "Hitsville,"
better known as Motown,
leading to the showdown
with white music.

But there was no showdown,
just the chorus of black and white
fighting for what was right.

And the music changed across our land
while our hands touched for the very first time.

It was about the good
that helped us all be better.

No more going back.

All the while there are other glories:
we know their stories in this tough city:
Pistons, Tigers, Lions, and Red Wings,
their victories and defeats.

And we love them anyhow.

A different day,
our guys won and were triumphant,
and in their way gave us that special moment
when we *all* were one.

But long seething rage and resentment
lay just below the surface.

July 23, 1967, the city exploded.
What was the purpose?

While white neighborhoods were quiet
the Motor City was engulfed in its worst riot.

Five days of fury.
Black snipers and others fought the cops
while looters ransacked and burned the shops.

National Guard and state police
struggled mightily to impose the peace, but
failed until the rioters were outnumbered.

43 dead, more than a thousand wounded.

A 4-year-old black girl, not a shooter,
shot dead because a cop thought - she's a looter.

This was the longest of our "Long Hot Summers."

Two thousand buildings destroyed,
millions in damages,
families displaced,
the city disgraced
for having abused and neglected its
black brothers and sisters.

45 years later,
Detroit still rotting, decay and corruption,
there was no interruption
of the downward spiral.
Not a shred of decency –
facing total bankruptcy.

We were "Murder City,"
no one took pity,
not the Governor nor the lawmakers.

This once fine city on the brink of total collapse,
so bad it thought to sell its treasures.
Would they strip works by Rivera
and others from another era
just to grab the cash?

Then by some miracle a civic partnership was forged.
Homeboy Dan Gilbert pumped his billions into downtown.

Though that's not enough to go around…
it *is* a start.

The Motor City's coming back.

Not fueled by cars,
but courageous acts
of entrepreneurs, artists
and other dreamers.
The schemers who know their aim is true.

They're white, and black, and brown
who had the guts to stick around
or take a chance to come long distance
to a place that's known great resistance
to growth, and hope, and change.
They bring their grit and their persistence.

Yes, DEE-TROIT is rising from the ashes.
Its gleaming downtown,
not stark glass and steel,
but Art Deco very real,
built from genuine commitment.

Live/work lofts that draw the young
to a present that is hung
on fresh ideas and capital.

We never gave up,
we never gave in.

Still, more folks must begin to be uplifted,

responsibility not shifted
from the mayor, city council, and businesspeople.

This rising tide must leave no one behind.
Our leaders must not be blind
to the needs of the poor and destitute.

We'd be wise
to remember while clearing lots
that homes and shops that once receded
always will be needed.

Once there was no hope,
but we fought back.

And made doubters into liars.

We're DEE-TROIT, baby, versus EVERYBODY!

By Michel Lynn Inaba

Michel Inaba wrote her first poem when she was a young teen. It was a tribute to her infant cousin who was born neurologically compromised.

She found that writing was useful for understanding her feelings and placing experiences, especially challenging ones, in perspective.

She has continued to write primarily for self-reflection, although she enjoys sharing her work within the writing community.

Michel majored in comparative literature at Indiana University and then switched her academic interest to psychology. She holds a master's degree in school psychology and a doctorate in developmental psychology.

She uses writing as a therapeutic tool in her practice as a psychologist and teaches meditation in the community.

Street Flowers

They look more than familiar,
cellophane-wrapped blooms stacked
flat and still. Flowers crushing flowers.
They were meant to stand and face the sun,
absorbing radiance thrown off by firestorms,
their proud heads bowed only in a rain's deluge,
or after the moon has drawn a curtain of night.
These blooms were harvested not for love,
but to assuage grief, to buoy the stricken
spirit of the innocent who had never walked
the survivor's path, who now traces the long
steps home after witnessing a gun's hot death,
stopping only to reach for mercy in a merchant's
bucket of flowers. Bound stem to stem, these are
working flowers, offering salve to a wounded soul.
Do not leave them at the make-shift shrine,
the beribboned fence, the gum-pocked sidewalk
marking horror. Take them home with you.
Tear off the wrap so they can breathe and finally drink.

Then cherish them, cherish them for as long
as they hold life.

By Richard Vestnys

Richard Vestnys, D.D., M.C.S., M.C., S.S.C.W., a poet, composer, theologian, master carpenter, chaplain, and retired chorister, has held memberships in several poetry, music, woodworking, and theological societies.

His published works include *No Greater Love*, through Abbey Book Bindery; *The Best of the Foliate Oak*, through the University of Arkansas, Monticello School of Arts and Humanities; and *Mountain of God* under the imprint of Laud Hall Seminary Press.

Relentless Sea

a sad sea
washes over me
relentless tide
will not subside
from deep to deep
these tears I weep
for you have died
I mourn and cried
a promised pain
like fallen grain
I miss you friend
this shall not end
just as the roil
against the soil
is always one
under the sun
so is my love
now up above
and there for thee
my joy will be
with you at last
'til waves have passed

Karen Durham

By Karen Durham

After toiling in the nonprofit world for many years, Karen decided to follow full time her vocation as a writer of fiction, creative non-fiction, and poetry.

Her work has been published in the *American River Review,* the *Writers on the Air* radio show and blog, and *California Update.*

As a member of the California Writer's Club, she has participated on a California Writers Week speaking panel and received honors for her short-fiction in competition sponsored by the club's Sacramento Branch.

She attends writing conferences several times each year. She hosts a Sacramento Shut Up and Write session (meetup.org), participates in a critique group, and takes poetry as well as memoir/creative non-fiction classes.

When not writing, Karen rejects advice to "Act your age." She runs, bicycles around town, swims, practices yoga & Pilates, eating & drinking with friends & spoiling her pets. She's thankful every day for all the wonderful people in her life.

Altitude Dementia

Write at sea level.

It's evident we can't breathe
up high where there's—no—
—air—where there's no there—there—where
our air is so spare we—gasp

Sounds like storms at sea.
I lay in sand crusted doze
lulled by sun-bleached shoreline warmth
into dangerous sleep—or
is it the cat's rumbling purr?

Do fish really float
after they die from drowning?
how ironic, if—
I wish I could use this trick
to protect me from myself.

Champion
Ken

By Kenneth R. Champion

Ken is the author of I*mages: A Collection of Poetry, Prose and More*. His writing is enriched by his 30 years combined service as a member of the U.S. Navy and the U.S. Coast Guard Reserve, as well as his 35 years as an associate transportation planner with the California Department of Transportation. In the 1960s, Ken was a member of the Nevada Jack and the Blue Canyon Gang, a western acting group.

Together with his wife, Linda Champion, Ken is the owner of Champion Writing Creations, LLC.

In addition to his poetry, Ken is an accomplished musician, playing both trumpet and harmonica with other local musicians as well as providing musical touches to his wife's fairy tales.

Ken and Linda have made numerous television appearances. They also can be seen on YouTube and TSPNTV.

The Ghost Town

As miners explored the gold fields of the Old West and moved from one gold strike area to the next, various towns popped up and grew. But others were left behind as the mines "played out" and people moved on to be with relatives or the next gold discovery. These situations created ghost towns.

With saloon doors cracked and creaking in the eerie, desert sun,

stands a solemn, lost remnant of how the West was won.
Lurking, silent shadows stare out behind old panes,
while tumbleweeds roam everywhere around the dusty plains.
Rustic, weathered buildings remind me of the past,
when life was very precious, and life was not so fast.
The hitching rails line ol' Main Street and lead to the livery stable,
while legends haunt its history with stories --- fact or fable?
Blowing dust and clattering shutters greet me as I search,
for signs of ol' Doc Holiday at the corral beyond the church.
And, a faded sign of "Boss of the Road" overalls contrasts against the sky,
near a broken-down old train station with a rusty old shoo-fly.
Walking down the street of time toward the general store,
made me sense that time of old – filled with Western lore.
At other times on windy days, bar room sounds arouse
sleeping spirits from their graves to party and carouse.
Jingling bottles and tinkling glasses rattle off the bar,
as playful, shadowy figures are sighted from afar.
And noisy sounds emerge, from the dark, old, drab saloon,
while distant player piano pounds out a lively tune.

Squinting at the barroom scene, a glowing apparition,
is downing shots of Red Eye with abandon and precision.
Then suddenly, aware of my stare, the phantoms of the past
turned and streaked toward me and left me all aghast!
With steely eyes and a laughing taunt, "Eeeh—hah, hah, hah!"
I cowered in fear and fell,
while shrieking spirits blew past me in this smokey scene from hell.
Then the ghostly figures from the past vaporized from the room,
while the piano still played on that Golden Slippers tune.
Shaken as I wandered from the surrealistic scene,
I shuddered with remembrance of the grisly, grinning dream,
of my sudden, stark appearance disrupting their routine,
from daily hunting parties with their ghostly, ghoulish theme.
So, if you plan to visit old towns that dot the West,
then be prepared for visits from uninvited guests,
the kind that come to visit when Boot Hill comes alive.
So, think it over tourists, before making that next drive.
May they rest in peace!

By Susan Dlugach

Before reporting news for the *Las Vegas Daily Optic* in New Mexico, Susan Dlugach earned a journalism degree from the University of Texas at Austin.

She also taught English in New Mexico and California while scribbling stories and poetry for herself.

Writing retreats and workshops are among her vacation destinations as she continues to hone her craft.

She's published in *California Update* and participates in poetry readings and a critique group.

Not to be a one-trick pony, she also enjoys music, dancing, yoga, hiking and studies Spanish with the hope of someday conversing easily and reading novels in that beautiful language.

Un Milagro

Argentina, Salta de la tierra was my destination from
Bolivia. I meandered south through the Andes from Tarija by
cab that Oscar drove, *un hombre amable,*
divorciado, as it seems many I met were.
El Rio Bermejo *en la*
frontera between those neighbors …
Gaucho land, another accent, me
hablando in my broken way,
improving my tongue syllable by syllable, not at
jet speed, *¡Paciencia!*
Kindness, much kindness there …
language builds bridges … *y un*
milagro celebrating no more earthquakes,
natives honor *la virgen* for this,
offer prayers, carnations, *los*
peregrinos walk miles and miles *a la catedral,* a
quest each year, sober, holy, fingering
rosaries in crowded streets of
Salta, now that the earth doesn't
tremble, shake, rattle or roll.
United in faith, gratitude to *la*
virgen whom they
worship as the mother of mothers
x-citement muted by sanctity
yearning to keep their
zone earthquake free.